WYLDBLOOD

ISSUE 17

Wyldblood Magazine #17 - December 2025

© 2025 Wyldblood Press and contributors.
Print ISBN-978-1-914417-23-8

Publisher: Wyldblood Press, Thicket View, Bakers Lane, Maidenhead SL6 6PX UK. www.wyldblood.com **Editor:** Mark Bilsborough. Single issues available worldwide via Amazon and from
wyldblood.com/shop

Submissions: we are regularly open for submissions of flash fiction, short stories and novels – check our website for our current status and requirements. We are a paying market. We also need artwork, people to review us, and people to review *for* us. Email
contact@wyldblood.com

Wyldblood 18 will be out in June 2026

Editorial

Mark Bilsborough

Hello again. It's been a while, but we've just managed to sneak in a second *Wyldblood Magazine* before the end of the year, and here it is. We have eight stories for you this time around, and fine ones they are too. As always it's a mix of science fiction and fantasy, both firmly grounded. We start with a Christmas tale (apologies if you're reading this in June) by Karl Dandenell, who around about now also has a novella coming out called *Between the Stars*, which is well worth tracking down. We continue with a fine story about a run-down café that's definitely not what it first seems by Rhoda Neville, before moving on to an edgy fantasy tale by Deborah L. Davitt, with river spirits and harsh realities. We then crank it up with DJ Cockburn's story about monsters, real or imaginary before sliding into sci-fi with Rob Gillham's dark story of interrogation and negotiation. Hugh McCormack's chilling sci-fi story about the unintended consequences of 'helpful' technology is next, followed by a small-town horror tale from Quinn J. Graham We finish up with a science fiction story by Wyldblood regular Liam Hogan on long life and lasting feuds.

Why the long gap? Life, mainly, but like many small press magazines we've been buffeted by all sorts of goings-on that have impacted our ability to get our stories into the world. And we're still working it out – so, for instance, we won't be able to ship paper copies of anything to the US for a while until we find a way to sort out the tariff situation which both wipes out our margins and adds a ton of paperwork to our lives (you can still buy through Amazon though). And we need to find new readers to make all of this cover its costs (yes, no yachts on the Caribbean for us) so spread the word, please, and don't be surprised to find us cropping up in unexpected places. If anyone wants to volunteer to join our marketing and sales team (paid in love, gratitude and deep kindness, but no actual money), our door is wide open.

We've started cranking up the website too, as I'm sure some of you have seen. New stories and some classics from back issues never before free and online are beginning to pop up, and we're aiming for a fresh story every week.

We've also changed our size this issue – gone smaller but fatter. That's mainly so the magazines can more easily fit on bookshelves – there's something inherently disposable about a magazine format, and since we're essentially an anthology of stories it makes sense to go for a format that makes them easier to stack alongside the ones already on your shelves, though we can't resist being slightly bigger than a standard paperback. Let us know what you think of the more compact package.

I could bang on about the evils of AI or the challenging politics that are sucking much of everyone's energy at the moment but there are stories to read, and, frankly, we kind of editorialise though our story choices. So I'll shut up and leave you to dive in. Stories at the front, book reviews at the back. Enjoy.

Mark

'Twas the Week Before Christmas

Karl Dandenell

'Twas the week before Christmas, and I wasn't stirring. I was getting right pissed.

The Joint was the oldest, cheapest bar in Watertown, New York. People minded their own business and simply drank. I liked that. Everything was smoke-stained and faded: the wallpaper, the vinyl booths, the barstools. Even the neon on the Schlitz beer sign pushed out a tired glow. And forget about music: there was neither jukebox nor radio. Nothing but low conversation and rumination.

Tonight my thoughts were focused on the Veil, and how I hated being on this side of it, especially in December. Pushing through snow drifts when you're three feet tall was a royal pain in the arse. "Frank," I said, tapping my empty glass. "Two fingers if you please."

"He means a shot," said the soldier to my left. "Two fingers is barely a thimble with your tiny hands, Santa's Little Helper." He smirked at his companions, who drunkenly giggled at his witticism. With their freshly pressed uniforms and buzz cuts, I guessed they were recently minted Fort Drum recruits, enjoying a last hurrah before Korea.

Even standing atop my barstool, I barely reached the other men's chins. The sheer fog of Burma Shave rolling off them made my eyes water. Definitely fresh meat from boot camp. "What's your name, boy?" I said, flipping my red hat's long tassel over my shoulder.

"Mike Harrison. What's it to you?"

"Well, *Private* Michael Harrison," I said, "Frank here understands both vernacular and context, so he is unlikely to give me the wrong pour based on my physiology. An arse like you, on the other hand, might require explicit directions when it comes to filling a glass."

Harrison slowly parsed the sentence and frowned. "You've got a big mouth there, shorty. Be careful someone doesn't shut it for you."

"Hey, hey, don't need no trouble tonight, Pádraig." Frank cracked open a new bottle of Jameson's, topping off my glass. "There you go." His voice held the confidence and calm of a man with two sawed-off shotguns in easy reach.

"*Sláinte*." I tossed back the whiskey. Water of life. Days like this I wanted to drown.

The bartender turned to Harrison. "What are you drinking, son?"

"Rheingold. In a bottle."

"I could never bring myself to drink beer that looked the same coming and going." Pulling a quarter from my waistcoat, I rolled it across my knuckles. "However, to each his own. And seeing how it's nearly Christmas, let me stand you a drink."

"What about my squad-mates?"

"The more, the merrier. Can't imagine you'll be getting much Rheingold around Pusan." I stacked a few coins on the bar and climbed down my stool with care, mindful of my balance. Even with my constitution, six drinks was pushing it. "I'm off, Frank, before the snow starts. No rest for the wicked in the Bey & Thomas toy department, leastways not 'til Sunday." I headed for the door, paused, and belted out in my strong tenor:

Now Dasher! Now Dancer! Now Prancer and Vixen!
On Comet! On Cupid! On Donder and Blixen!

Once outside, I buttoned up my wool coat, pulled on my gloves, and hunkered down in the alley, becoming just another shadow cast by the old iron streetlamp.

Fat, wet flakes drifted down. I shifted a bit, wishing I had of those fancy Thermos bottles from the kitchen department right about then. A swallow of tea or even watery American coffee would be welcome. Still, this was nothing compared to Boston last January. I shivered with the memory.

I'd nearly frozen my bollocks off hiding in the river while St. Nick's agents combed the shore looking for free leprechauns like my Whelan and me. I hoped my nephew had gotten away, even if the kid's stupid mouth had cost us half our score. What could I do? When my sister lay on her deathbed, I swore I'd keep an eye on the boy. His father had already been taken by the elves, may they choke on lumps of coal.

An hour later, the bar disgorged Harrison and his squad of wannabe Audie Murphys. I grinned and whispered a charm. Not the best idea, perhaps, but I was cold and stiff and still a little buzzed. Besides, it was just a *wee* phantasm of greasy hamburgers and fries.

Harrison stopped and sniffed the air while the other soldiers headed toward the bus stop. "I'll catch you guys back at base." Then he turned down the alley toward an all-night diner. As soon as the sidewalk cleared, I emerged from the shadows. "Someone's been a naughty boy," I whispered, and slammed into Harrison's knees.

The soldier managed a girlish shriek as he tumbled into the gritty snow. I clamped a hand on his nose and mouth and showed him the six-inch obsidian blade I'd picked up in New York after some punks mugged me at the docks. Cold steel gave me the collywobbles but flaked stone bothered me not a whit. And it was sharp as a surgeon's blade.

"It's a big mouth you got there, sir, and you'd be wise to keep it shut. Blink twice if you understand."

He nodded, flinching as the knife nicked him.

"I said blink, ya eejit." I shook my head. "Let's get something straight, okay? I'm a *leprechaun*, not an elf. Just because I'm dressed like some poxy Christmas helper doesn't mean I'm one of *them*. Not even close. Got it?"

Harrison blinked. Twice.

"You're learning. Good." Keeping the knife in place, I searched his pockets with my free hand, coming up with a wallet. I flipped it open to his driver's license. "Come up from Hoboken, I see."

"Take my money," Harrison whispered. "Please don't kill

me."

"Boy, I don't make widows for five dollars and a bus ticket. But I'll have that wedding ring."

"Please. It belonged to my grandfather."

"And now it belongs to me," I said, wiggling the knife. "Now give it over. *Please.*"

He worked the ring off, slowly. I put it between my teeth.

"That's some fine quality gold, that is," I said, tucking it away. "Now, what are we going to do with you?" As a rule, I never killed anyone unless my back was against the wall. And Harrison wasn't a threat—the way he winced when he moved his leg told me he'd probably twisted something. Poor kid. Just a stupid boy who got schooled for mouthing off in a bar. We've all been there.

He flinched when I kissed him on the cheek. "There! All you have to do is lay there nice and quiet while I go on my way. May the road rise up to meet you."

With a kick, I launched myself, landed on my toes, and performed a bow worthy of Queen Tatiana's court. "Merry Christmas, Private Harrison!" Then I strolled away, whistling the opening bars of "The Wild Rover."

The next morning, I rose late from my cot, the metal frame creaking like an old man's bones. I tip-toed across the cold wood floor to the cupboard and retrieved the ceramic cookie jar I'd secreted behind a loose board. The jar was the color of melted butter and shaped like a fat chef, complete with *toque blanc* lid.

Harrison's wedding ring joined my stash of Double Eagles, Spanish doubloons, and Mexican gold pesos that I'd acquired in trade for watches, lockets, and other precious things.

I scooped my hands into the jar and let the coins drip through my fingers. Close. So close. Almost enough to bribe the dwarves who guarded Queen Tatiana's borders. *Bring us two stones' weight of gold*, they'd said. *And we won't turn you over to the elves.*

Two stones! That's robbery, pure and simple! I'd sputtered and cursed, while they leaned on their pickaxes and waited for me to run out of breath.

Two stones, leprechaun, repeated the older dwarf, before chucking me into a nearby bramble.

Saint Nick was putting the squeeze on everyone, it seemed.

I clanked the *toque blanc* back on the chef's head. The week before, when I was returning from a late night walk (and some light pickpocketing), I'd detoured through an empty lot and paid a visit to the old Hawthorne trees behind my boarding house. I'd once asked the landlady, Mrs. MacDiarmada, about the lot. She thought it the remains of some house that had burned down before the war. I knew different. It was a wild place, kept that way by my people. When I placed my hands on one of the Hawthorne trunks, I heard it sleeping, dreaming of spring. With the next full moon came round in a week, I was sure I could easily sing the trees awake and open a passage through the Veil.

And a good thing, too. Elves were nearing Watertown. I couldn't smell them, but I *felt* them. Pins and needles in my toes. A dryness in the throat. And dreams. Dreams of crawling across ice fields, chased by wolf howls and laughter.

For years, I'd crossed the Veil to pursue my mischief in the Irish countryside, as one does, but when that puffed-up bastard St. Nick needed magical labor for his North Pole factories, he sent his elves to snatch up any leprechaun, pixie, or gnome who ventured outside Queen Tatiana's realm. Santa was determined to slake the human children's growing hunger for toys at any cost.

Between elvish scouts and corrupt dwarves, I was cut off from home. Like many of my fellow fae, I'd chosen to flee the island.

I took jobs where I could, mainly working the carnival circuits and Christmas displays in tight-ass little towns across England and America, slowing gathering my stake so I could bribe my way back.

Damn dwarves. May their beards fall out in the middle of their supper.

On this side of the Veil, fae magic was barely strong enough to influence slow-witted human folk. And if we tried anything more than a minor cantrip, elvish hunting parties would come running, stinking of cloves and cardamon. So fae moved often and generally avoided each other, lest word get back to Santa.

But I wouldn't be looking over my shoulder much longer. I was short maybe two hundred coins, a month's work if I set my mind to it. Once I had that gold, I'd show the human realm my backside. Let someone else steal their chickens or sour the milk. Nothing on this side of the Veil was worth getting chained to a workbench, making dolls and wooden trains for *him*.

Footsteps creaked on the stairs. I quickly hid the cookie jar and put on a robe I'd stolen from the children's department. Navy blue terrycloth.

There was a knock. "Are you decent, Mr. Lynch?"

I raised my voice, mindful of my landlady's poor hearing. "I am more than decent, Mrs. MacDiarmada. I am excellent!"

The door opened, admitting a very thin, very bent-over woman whose white hair was done up in a tight bun. Her apron of white and yellow daisies was ironed within an inch of its life. "You make me laugh, Mr. Lynch." She handed me a cup of strong tea and a plate with toast cut into triangles. "I was making myself breakfast and thought you might like a cuppa."

"You're a blessing, you are." I set the dishes on the end table that served as my coffee table. "Oh. As long as you're here, I have the rent." I snapped my fingers, producing a fan of dollar bills.

"It's not due for another week, Mr. Lynch. Still, I won't say no." The money disappeared into the daisy field.

I slurped my tea. "I hope to be visiting family for the holidays." And never coming back.

"Good for you. Though I imagine the toy department will be frightfully busy until the last minute."

"Every day is busy day for a Santa's Helper," I said. "Speaking of which, I really should finish this lovely meal and catch my bus."

"Then I won't keep you," said Mrs. MacDiarmada. She picked up the newspaper from the floor and shuffled toward the trash. "Oh, you had a visitor yesterday. I meant to tell you but I was asleep by the time you came home."

"Mmmm?" I said around a mouthful of toast.

"He said he was a nephew of yours from Sligo. Or was it Cork?

Anyway, I told him you were working and he should come back later. Didn't think it proper to have him wait here by himself."

"Not proper at all." Sudden sweat trickled down my ribs. "Did he give his name?"

"I'm sure he did, but for the life of me I can't remember." She dropped the newspaper in the waste basket. "He certainly looked like a relation."

"Another handsome gentleman with green eyes?"

"Listen to you, Mr. Lynch. I mean he was round and not particularly tall. Like yourself." She turned to go.

"Thank you, Mrs. MacDiarmada." I closed the door behind her and coughed against a piece of bread stuck in my throat. "Well, bugger."

I was rushing out of the house, pulling up my green tights when I spied a bright red envelope tucked under the mat. The front was blank except for my name written in block letters. Inside, I found a Norman Rockwell "Home for Christmas" card and a short message:

I think the Red Coats are in town. Can we meet?
—W

Whelan! I scanned the street but saw only Mr. Jenkins scraping the ice from the windshield of his Ford Mainline wagon.

I stuffed the card into my coat and bolted for the bus stop, heedless of the icy sidewalk. Fortunately for me, the bus was running late, and I found a seat by the back door. Every time we stopped to pick up passengers, I gripped my knife tightly, alert to anyone wearing hand-stitched red coats or white fur collars. Fecking elves. And fecking Whelan – he always did have the worst timing.

On the other hand, another set of hands *might* be useful right about now.

My thoughts were interrupted by a small boy in the seat in front of me, who stuck out his tongue, then tried to engage me in a staring contest. I produced a candy cane. "May I, ma'am?" I asked the women sitting next to the boy. She looked up from her knitting, took in my costume, and nodded.

"I hope you've been good this year, boy," I said, handing over the candy. "Because Santa," I whispered, "can be really horrid when he wants to be."

I got off at the next stop.

"Looks like a good crowd today," said Phil, strapping on an extra-large pillow. He was thinner than the last Santa, and smelled of onions and vodka.

"Yeah, sure." I fiddled with my itchy fake ears, tucking the wire frame under my hat. Some petty part of me wanted to leave them in my locker and replace them with a proper glamour. With elves nearby, though, I needed to control those impulses. *Magic attracts magic*, as the saying goes. I'd gotten lucky with that charm in the alley. "Hey, Phil, be a good soul and loan us your flask."

"Tough night, eh?" He rummaged around his locker.

"Tough morning." The vodka was as harsh as expected. Even though Bey & Thomas paid the seasonal staff a decent wage, we wouldn't get our final checks (and the promised bonuses) until December 26, and Phil was probably skating along on nickels from the tip jar. "Cheers, mate." I took a second pull and returned the flask. Then I pushed my hat down firmly and stuck a candy cane in the corner of my mouth. "Time to make some memories, fat man."

On a normal day, I'd stand at the front of the queue, chatting with mothers and fathers, quietly shepherding the children onto Santa's lap or over to the Santa's Workshop photo booth.

Today, though, I didn't say much. My thoughts churned between those damn elves and Tatiana's crooked border guards. Caught between the devil and deep blue sea, I was.

"Come on, Patrick, show us the happy elf!" said the photographer.

My expression was more grim than grin but the photographer snapped anyway.

Then it was back to the queue, the children excited and tired, frightened or nose-running sick. We finally got a break when Phil decided Santa needed a smoke. I put up the **Feeding the reindeer—back in a few minutes** sign, and we parked themselves on the back stairs. Phil lit up a king-size Chesterfield and offered me one.

"More of a pipe man, myself," I said with a shake of my head. "Phil, can I ask you something?"

"Sure thing."

"If you needed money in a hurry, say, a *lot* of money, what would you do?"

"I'd play the ponies." Phil flicked ash from his beard. "You can make a good score on the Daily Double if you're lucky."

"My luck hasn't been good lately," I said. And throwing down a strength charm on a racehorse would be like lighting a signal fire for any hunters.

Phil took a final drag. "There's always the pawn shop on Oak Street. They pay less but don't ask questions."

"I've already sold everything I can." Including the silver candlesticks I'd found in the back of Mrs. MacDiarmada's closet.

"Well, as my ex-wife used to say, if you can't pay the bill, make friends with someone who can." The Chesterfield became a shooting star down the stairwell. "Back to the North Pole."

As soon as my shift was over, I grabbed my coat and headed down the escalator, taking the opportunity to jostle a well-dressed woman holding a stack of brightly wrapped packages. I apologized profusely and helped her to a nearby chair. Then, with further apologies, I collected her scattered boxes. The floor manager, Mr. Peavey, brought her a paper cup of water. I used the distraction to liberate the woman's billfold from her Kelly bag. Every bit helped.

The biting wind nearly tore my knit hat off as I cleared the revolving doors. When I reached the corner, I tracked a huge mass of storm clouds pushing their way from the east. This cheered me: a good dose of sleet might obscure my trail.

A prickle like tiny mice feet ran down my back. I casually turned in a circle, searching the shadows. After a moment, I spied a familiar figure huddled behind the newspaper stand.

"Whelan!"

The leprechaun who stood up wore a stained overcoat missing several buttons. It flapped in the wind, exposing the cheap wool suit underneath. He offered me a chilly hand to shake. "Well met, uncle. You get my card?"

"Aye," I said. "How'd you track me down?"

"I remembered you mentioning Watertown a few years back, and it didn't take long to find a boarding house run by an Irish grandmother," said Whelan. "Getting a wee predictable in your old age."

"And yet I'm still here. What can I do for you, ya little shite?" He wasn't that much shorter than me, but he was a few decades younger.

"I need a place to lay low. Two North Pole bastards almost netted me in Buffalo not a fortnight ago. Only stayed ahead of them by hitching a ride on the back of a vegetable truck. Ate nothing but turnips and carrots for two days."

"That must have been hard."

"Wasn't so bad," said Whelan. "The bed was open to the sky, and I could smell the farms as we passed. If I closed my eyes, I could imagine I was back home, tying the goats' tails together with invisible twine."

I squeezed his shoulder. "You think they followed you?"

He blew on his hands. His gloves were torn and dirty. "They're close, uncle. I can feel it in my bones." He fixed an eye on me. "Bet you can, too."

"A bit," I admitted. More than I liked. "Come on, best we don't dally." I pointed to an approaching streetcar and we jumped on after the other passengers, worming our way past packages and bulging shopping bags.

Whelan put his head close and switched to Gaelic. "I wouldn't impose on you if it weren't serious, Pádraig. You know that."

"It's always serious," I responded in the same language.

"What do you need?"

"Just a place to catch my breath. Swear on my mother."

"Uh, uh. And if I happen to have a few coins to spare, you wouldn't say no," I said.

Whelan padded his breast. I heard the soft jingle of coins. "I'm doing all right, thank you. But I could always use a little local currency. Conductors can't make change for a sovereign."

"Here." I passed over a twenty I'd acquired from the Bey & Thomas customer. "That will get you a ticket someplace warmer."

"You're a blessing." He stuffed the bill into a shirt pocket. "You know, until just recently, I was getting together a big stake. Truth be told."

I sighed. "What happened this time?"

He frowned. "I bought my way into a regular dice game in Brooklyn. Kept coming back every week, winning a little, losing a little. Then one night some flashy fellow in a blue-striped Zoot suit starts throwing down bundles of cash like he'd robbed a bank and couldn't wait to spend it."

"And you decided to improve your luck," I said.

"Just a little. A nudge. Then the money got so big I couldn't help myself. I hit it with everything I had and came up three sevens in a row." He rubbed his nose. "Before I could count the pot, the elves dropped through the skylight like it was someone's chimney on the 24th. Everybody thought it was the peelers, and Mr. Zoot pulled out a horrible great pistol. Everyone grabbed for the cash and I had to bust out a window to get away."

"That's rough," I said. "But you brought it on yourself, you eejit."

"I know. I know."

I put an arm around him. As much as Whelan frustrated me at times, I had to admit it was good to see family. "Are you hungry?"

"I could eat cold soup without a spoon."

"I think we can do better than that," I said.

The sleet had begun in earnest by the time we reached the house.

"Mrs. MacDiarmada?"

There was no answer. Perhaps she was out doing her last-minute shopping, buying toys for her grandchildren. I wondered how she'd feel if she knew those colorful toys were churned out by imprisoned fae?

"Wait in the sitting room," I said. "Keep your feet off the furniture." Everything was covered in crocheted blankets.

I stole upstairs and retrieved my cookie jar, wrapping it in my terrycloth robe and tying it all into a neat bindle. I wanted to be ready in case Whelan went along with my plan.

The wind sounded like wolves.

When I came downstairs, I found him spreading his coat over the radiator. "Nice place."

"Keeps me dry," I said. I set my bindle on the couch. "Why don't you rest a moment while I make us some sandwiches. I think there's roast beef leftover from Sunday."

"Sounds grand."

I went to the kitchen, put out a couple of plates, and piled them with slices of cold meat, cheese, and bread. I filled the kettle and set it on the white porcelain stove to boil. The gas was fussy, as usual. As I was lighting my third match, I felt a twinge of familiar magic, like someone tugging at my ear.

I slipped back into the hallway and peered into the sitting room. Whelan was sitting in the dark, his feet on the sofa. "Did you hear anything?"

"Nothing but the wind." He retrieved his coat and put it on.

"Come on, then, let's eat." I took my bindle to the kitchen and set it next to the table. The bathrobe had definitely been re-tied. And was it lighter?

Whelan tucked in without ceremony. I took a few bites, my appetite suddenly gone.

"Nephew," I said.

"Yes?"

"I'm tired of this. Aren't you?"

He wiped his mouth on a kitchen towel. "What?"

"This," I said. "Putting a stake together. Every time one of us gets close to having enough gold, the elves almost catch us and we have to leave it behind, or we lose it in a craps game, or someone straight up grifts us, like that pixie in Canada."

He tried hard not to look at my bindle, but I saw his glance. "Yeah, she pulled the wool over our eyes, she did."

"I think it's time to pool our resources," I said. "Give me your gold."

"What?" he said. "If this is your idea of hospitality, I'll find somewhere else to hide." He climbed out of this chair.

"Whelan, sit down."

"I'll stand, thank you."

"Then at least listen," I said. "If you loan me your gold, I'll have enough to pay the bribe and then — ."

"Then I'll be stuck here, only poorer. No, thank you, Pádraig. I'm sorry about Boston but I'll not dance to this tune."

"Whelan," I spoke quietly. "I know what you did in the sitting room."

"So I put my feet on the furniture, big deal!"

"I've known you since you were born, ya gobshite," I said, setting the bindle on the table. With a twist, I untied the robe. Under the chef's toque blanc lay a double handful of lead subway tokens. "You think I wouldn't recognize one of your charms?"

"I was desperate, Pádraig," he said with a sniff. "I haven't see home in so long, I can barely dream about it."

I nodded. "I know the feeling. But we're leprechauns. We don't steal from *family*." I scooped out the tokens and held out my hand. Whelan rolled up his pants, revealing two heavy wool socks tied outside his garters. With a hangdog expression, he emptied their contents into the cookie jar: gold coins and Harrison's wedding ring.

"Now," I said, "if you give me the rest, you'll be home in eight days."

He frowned and crossed his arms. "How?"

"Once I cross the Veil, I'll take two stones' worth of gold from my own stash and wait for you at the border. Just make sure you come through the same place I do. Otherwise, we might miss each other."

He considered it. "I don't know. Why do I have to wait eight days?"

"It'll be December 26," I said. "The Red Coats will be home and you can open the Veil without worry."

"Swear it, Pádraig." Whelan spit in his palm. "Swear on Queen Titania."

"I swear." I spit in my own palm and grasped his. "Long may She reign."

Whelan wiped his hand on his trousers, then pulled a kerchief from his pocket. Inside lay a thin gold bar. "Will this be enough?"

I hefted the bar and nodded. Just enough. "Follow me."

We headed out the back door.

"Once I'm gone, get yourself over to The Joint and ask for Frank." I told him the address. "Give him that twenty and tell him you want to rent your uncle's old room. It's not much—just a cot in a storeroom—but no one will bother you."

The wind abruptly shifted direction, and moonlight stabbed down through an opening in the clouds. The air grew colder and I smelled cinnamon and cloves. *Oh no.*

"Run!" I took off, the bindle banging against my back. I crossed the street and ran for the Hawthorne ring, Whelan hard on my heels.

"What?!

"The elves must have been closer than we thought," I said, puffing.

We reached the trees. "Was it my charm? Did they sense it?" said Whelan.

"Yes." I shut my eyes and spoke the ancient words, willing the tree to wake.

"Pádraig!"

"I know!" *There.* The Veil opened. On the other side, a young sika hind pawed at the dirt, its white spots glowing in the moonlight. I turned, and my grin crashed when I saw Whelan staring through the Veil. Tears coursed down his cheeks.

In that moment, I knew. I knew in my bones he wouldn't make it. After I left, he'd just stand there, gawping, transfixed by the site of *home*.

And the elves would snatch him up and take him to the North Pole, just like his father.

Someone approached from the opposite direction, crying rage and fury. I heaved my bindle to Whelan. "Here. Take it and go!"

His caught it, barely. "But—"

"And if you're not there waiting for me next week, well, you'll wish you'd never been born. Go!"

Whelan put a foot into the circle. "I'll be there, uncle, I swear. Thank you! Thank you! I'm sorry!" In two steps he was gone.

"*Eejit.*" I ran. Harder than a deer chased by hounds, I ran toward The Joint and Frank's shotguns, the hunters close behind me. That'd be a fine surprise for them.

Even if I didn't make it, I still had my knife. If the elves wanted me, it would cost them more than gold.

I ran.

Karl Dandenell is a graduate of Viable Paradise and a Full Member of the Science Fiction & Fantasy Writers Association. He and his family, plus their feline overlords, live on an island near San Francisco famous for its Victorian architecture and low-speed traffic. Karl has published over 50 works of short fiction in the United States, Canada, and Great Britain. Follow his occasional posts @karldandenell.bsky.social and read more about of his fiction at www.firewombats.com.

Greasy

Rhoda Neville

On the day that Mary started conversing with thin air, we began to worry. She'd always been one to mumble to herself. Over the years, we'd grown used to that, but now she was really holding forth.

'No,' she said as she backed through the swinging door that separates the kitchen from the dining room, a tray of clean cutlery in her hands. 'You may as well stop fretting. It'll never happen!'

Adam and I looked at each other across the busy floor of the Victory. Her tone was so natural, she might have been talking into an earbud. Only thing was, Mary didn't 'hold with such truck.' She was an old-fashioned sort, preferring the landline to mobiles and snail mail to the other. I was worried her age was causing her to lose it a little.

She turned and saw us staring at her. 'Here,' she said, pushing the tray towards Adam, 'Take a load off an old lady!' He grabbed the tray, wheeled around, and stuck it under the counter.

By now, everyone in the caff was watching us. All the regulars had seen Mary, and heard her, chatting away but never so blatantly as just now. She was the fixture here, the queen-pin, and at near eighty her customers and staff alike watched her for signs of wear and tear. She didn't work the dining floor as often as she used to and she left most of the heavy lifting to Adam and me, but she still came in seven to six, on six days a week. On Sundays, we didn't open.

'Mare, what's going on?' John was the only person who called her that name, like she was a horse, and we were pretty sure that he's the only one she'd allow it from. He was a few months her senior and thinking of giving up work as a ceramics teacher. Only thinking about it, as he came in every weekday for his late breakfast, Number 2, before heading off to the salt mines of tutelage.

She waved a bony brown hand. 'Nothing John, just mind your p's and q's, why don't you?'

He snorted and went back to stirring his coffee, like he'd done a good job, like he'd performed a daily ritual.

She gave us all a dark look and stamped through the door into the kitchen again.

Adam shrugged and went back to his table of construction workers. I finished writing down a barrister's order for a Number 3 and took the chit to the kitchen window. Raoul, on the other side of the partition, was flipping and grilling while Mary filled an order for a Number 6, the muesli and yoghurt selection.

Raoul raised their eyebrows at me. With her back turned Mary said, 'Enough of that you two. I'm not round the bend, yet.'

Roaul doubled down on the frying, and I turned back to the dining room. As I pivoted away, Mary added, 'Daphne, you're the floor manager. Go manage it.'

That was weird. She'd given me that title four years ago, right after Jack died, and then never gave me free reign to act on it. She'd just carried on being the café whirlwind she'd always been, while taking on some of her husband's work. The only real change was she'd upgraded Raoul to cookie. Jack had been training them on and off for a couple of years before his sudden demise, almost like he'd suspected he'd drop dead of a heart attack one day.

Now, I looked around the well-worn interior of the café as if I was planning to do something managerial. There really wasn't much I could do. The customers were content, and we all knew how Mary felt about the place. Its original opening had predated her birth in some far-off Commonwealth country by twenty years, having been christened on the tail end of the Great War. I didn't guess much had changed since then. Well, that wasn't true. We had a modern cash register and a phone line and Wi-Fi, but we still only took cash.

I had to admit, I loved the interior with its wooden wainscoting and lime washed walls above. It had old prints from the street outside showing our area of London as it changed through the 20th century and a few newer photos from this millennium. The deal wood tables were bolted to the wall, and the chairs were a mish mash of whatever Jack and Mary had been able to buy from the local junk shops to replace the original ones when they couldn't be repaired any more. With the scattering of customers who'd come in before the lunch rush in their autumn wear, we might have been in any time. Like the door from the outside was a portal to 1942 or 1955, or maybe 1982.

On a management level, I wouldn't be allowed to change a thing about the place. Which was just as well, as I wouldn't want to.

The outside door opened, and a new customer (guest as Mary called them) blew in on a swirl of rain. With the big plate glass windows all steamed up, we were cut off from the weather, only finding out what it was doing with incoming clientele. This one was new. One of the hungry that seemed to be filling our streets more and more. She must have seen the red, hand-lettered sign perched in the window that read, 'Pay it forward here. We never turn a hungry person away.'

Like most of our first timers, she darted glances all about her. She had lanky hair that was probably blonde when it was washed, blue eyes that were blurred by confusion or drugs, and bone structure I would at one time have said I'd die for. She was thin, model-thin, basically emaciated. And her formerly stylish coat, a linen and silk number appliqued with soft blossoms, couldn't measure up against the October weather. *Might be dressed up for the catwalk*, I thought.

All the heads that had swivelled to stare as she walked in swivelled back to their business, quick-like. It's another thing I like about our crowd. They'll stare till their eyes bug out at a well-heeled stranger, but when one of the hungry walks in, they give them space. Some of them even contribute a few coins to the kitty.

I approached her, keeping enough distance between us not to start up her flight instinct, and asked her what she'd like.

'Do you have a carrot?' Her voice was timid.

'What if we make you a breakfast roll?'

'Oh, I shouldn't, really.' Her voice was soft, almost refined. She shot those keeks about the caff again, as if she thought someone might be judging her and her hands went to her concave stomach in an unconscious gesture.

'It's okay,' I said as the flash of an idea hit me. 'You'll fit in your dresses just fine.'

'I will?'

'You'll look grand!'

She nodded her head, a little clarity coming into her dazzled eyes. I jotted down the order and went to the window. 'Priority, Raoul.' They nodded, having seen our new guest.

When she was sat in a chair with a plate of egg on a bap and some fresh sliced carrots, a mug of tea beside her, I went looking for Mary. She was in the back office. I could hear her talking again as I approached so I rapped the door loudly.

I told her about the catwalk girl and she said, 'Poor lamb.'

'Aye. Do we have anything in the lost and found for her?' We went through the box of clothes we had for emergencies, and I came up with something that would keep her a shade warmer. 'Thanks Mary.'

'Not to worry, Daph.' As I pulled the door closed, I could hear her say, 'Yes, I told you she is one of the good ones. She'll maybe stay on when I'm gone.'

If I hadn't been in such a skuttle to get the clothes to the girl before she slipped off, I'd have been right back in there. As it was, I glanced through the narrowing gap between door and jamb and thought I saw the shadow of someone else in the room. Then, I could have sworn I heard another voice answer her back.

Concerned for the welfare of our new customer, I took the clothes out to the girl who was eating with a sort of frantic decorum. You could see she wanted to shovel it in as fast as she could, but long training made her nibble her food. She'd take one bite, then put the roll down between, masticating like she was counting chews. When she swallowed though, it was with that eagerness that I've seen in the hungriest ones. I wondered if she was anorexic. I wasn't sure if you could be both a half-starved homeless person and that.

The girl looked at the clothes I brought as if they were rags. Ironic, when what she was wearing was beginning to shred. I said, 'Look, these may not be the height of fashion, but you need to stay warm. It's getting' brutal out there.'

Her face cleared then and a beatific smile lighted her up. She said, 'Okay, thank you. I can wear them when I'm not working.' That voice was still as light as the first flakes of snow, but the food seemed to have put words back in her mouth. She laid her roll down again and accepted the pile, putting it on the chair beside her.

'Mind you put them on before you leave here.' Satisfied that I'd done what I could for her, my mind pinged back to Mary.

Adam was stacking clean glasses under the counter, and I sidled up to him. 'She's at it again.' It came out like a hiss, and I bit off the last word.

'Daph, don't be a tool. She's probably just working things out in her head. Y'know she's got everything to do.'

'That's what we're here for.'

'Well, you're the dining room manager. Do something about it.' He grabbed a jug with water in it and went round the tables. I left him to serving and went to Raoul.

'I'm worried about Mary,' I said. 'She seems like she's talking to herself in there, and then answering herself in other voices. Convincing ones, at that.'

'What you saying? You think she's loco?' They lifted the side of their mouth and concentrated on flipping some flat sausages. Then they turned liquid brown eyes to me and said. 'Woman, you're too fussy. She's never been nothing but good to us. Give her some space.' Okay, so I'd misinterpreted both my colleagues this morning.

And they were right. Adam had been a runaway, Raoul a fellow European until after Brexit, when we weren't supposed to be fellow anything anymore, and the kid who washed the dishes after school was on the edge of drug dependency until Mary had taken him on.

When Raoul was in danger of being deported, Mary had slogged through the paperwork with them. And me? Well, she helped me through the months and years of my transition. Before Jack passed, she'd turned a blind eye to my needs — well, not a blind eye, but she'd pretended not to notice that 'David' didn't sit right with me. She'd shielded me that way, so Jack never had to imagine David as Daphne. Kept me in my job. After that, she'd helped me through the hormonal tidal waves, the aches and pains, stared down any customer who looked at me sideways. She was gold, was Mary, like the Biblical staff and rod.

So, Adam and Raoul were right. What did I want to happen? Her carted away to some old folks' home? Nah. She's accepted us all as we were. Us and her 'guests.' Given us a place and support. It was the least I could do now. Let her be. Let her talk to her invisible friends.

I went back to the front. Saw that the catwalk girl was gone. She'd left a gift though. One of the appliqued flowers from her old coat. You could see she'd left it on purpose. The thread unpicked by hand. I marvelled that she could hold her fingers steady enough to do the job. As I cleared the table, I picked it up and put it in my apron pocket. It was as good as a thank you. Thought I might pass it on to Mary for her memory wall in the office.

The coffee crowd was being replaced by the lunch bunch filtering in, so I joined Adam in the business of our business. An hour and a half later, as the latest customers were seen to, a new group walked through the door.

Every week we have a few random customers, not only hungries like the catwalk girl, but complete strangers. People from outside our wee London backwater. But this lot stuck out like meerkats in a barrel of Siamese.

There were three of them, two Londoners and an American. They were all bundled up as the squall outside dictated, in versions of long peacoats, tweed and leather. They paused inside the door and removed them, and you could see that the Yank wore the regulation beard and Michael Caine hornrims, the plaid shirt with khaki braces, the well-cut jeans, and ankle high hushpuppies of his kind. He seemed a little old for the role, but I reckoned he was patient zero of the Hipster pandemic. He was talking as they entered, and his vowels put any doubt about his origin to rest. The other two were younger and they dressed in finer versions of 'chore' jackets, one with a spotted silk scarf hanging over his snug tee shirt, the other with an off-colour waistcoat. Man-buns in place. Trousers of the same fine quality as their jackets. Leather chelseas polished to a luscious sheen. Yuccies, for sure. Very natty and definitely not from around here.

Not that we're segregationists or anything. Our policy is come one come all, but these three set the tips of my ears tingling. They took their time looking for a table. Just stood gazing around at the high anaglypta clad ceiling, the walls faded to an organic green. They took in the deal tables, the eclectic chairs, and I was afraid they were going to like it here.

Our crowd, good as their form, were all inspecting these three. Some had downed their cutlery and stared in frank curiosity, others keeked out from under eyebrows, continuing to shovel food into their chops in a race to get back to their jobs. The incomers were oblivious.

I realised, eventually, that they were waiting to be seated. A snort escaped me as I went forward to them, squeezing the fabric flower in my pocket. 'Take a seat anywhere, gentlemen.'

'Oh, righty-ho,' one of the Londoners had a mouth full of plums, 'Is the window table available, then?'

'That'll park us a bad view,' the third man wasn't Eton educated. He scraped a chair across the tile floor and plonked down in it, while the others alighted with more decorum. 'Three of yer best plates, luv.'

I wasn't about to be given that sort of a herculean task, so I went to fetch menus. When I got back, they were muttering about the "bones" of the room and how they could "insert an RSJ when they knock into next door." I chucked the menus at them and told them to choose something.

Then, I went to the back for Mary. I was in such a flocht that I forgot to knock the door and pushed right through. I had the glimpse of a bunch of folk in the room with her, but as I blinked and looked around, I saw the office was empty. 'Mary, there's a trio of sharks out there, wanting to take over the caff!'

Mary, whose face had gone from surprise to outrage at me to outrage at what I was saying, snapped her mouth shut. She growled, 'I was wondering when they'd be around.'

She sprang her slight frame out of her swivel chair and came around the desk. 'See what I was tellin' you?' She cried at the room as she loosed and retied her apron, on the move.

I peeked over my shoulder as we left and saw a flicker of human faces. Attached to the faces were the impression of bodies, standing and sitting on every available surface. But I was swept up in her wake and followed her as she burst into the dining room.

The rest of the caff were pointedly minding their own business by now, though I could practically see their ears flapping as they strained to listen. The threesome had moved to a table near the centre of the room. I heard one say, 'You know these prices are ridiculous.'

'Yeah, def, first thing to change,' came the American voice.

Mary stalked to their table. 'I thought I told you I'm not interested.'

'Well, good morning to you as well, Ms Mary.' It was clear they knew each other already.

'This menu, luv, is chicken jalfrezi donkey kong.' His two mates looked quizzical until he added, 'You should really cut it down, Mary.'

'We manage. Why are you here?'

'We're peckish, thought we'd try out the local cuisine. Will that be a problem?'

Mary looked over her shoulder at me and I felt movement in the room as Adam took a step forward. But she held up her hand. 'No, I expect we can feed you.' She took her notepad out.

They hemmed and hawed for an overly long time discussing the selection, agreeing what to share and what sides they wanted for their own. Meanwhile, I could see our actual customers tuning up their ears, trying to hear it all. Mary stood, patient as a statue, watching them with unfriendly eyes. Finally, they ordered, and she brought the chit to Roaul. 'With extra olive oil,' she murmured. Then, she stood by the swing door, watching them from across the room. 'Be a love and take them their flatware, Daph.'

I did, and fitted the forks and knives around their tablets, which took up a good portion of the table. There was also with a card-mounted copy of what looked like a sterile mock-up of the room we were in. There were some floorplans on one of the tablets. My stomach turned to a lump of ice at the sight of it.

'Bring us some water for the table, there's a good… girl.'

I squeezed the flower again as I went for a jug and three glasses. After I poured, I went back to stand beside Mary. 'What's going on?'

Never taking her eyes off them, she said through the side of her mouth, 'The posh one and the East Ender came in late last week. You've heard of Pulverise?'

'That toffee nosed group of "gourmet coffee houses?"' My voice climbed a couple of octaves.

Mary nodded, 'They're front men for the conglomerate behind it. Want to set one up here. In the Vic.'

'But this is a regular working caff in a regular area, not *Shoreditch*! They'll never get their prices!' We both turned in surprise at Adam's outburst. He rarely uttered more than four words in a row when he wasn't dealing with customers.

'You'd think, but the tall one seems to believe there's gentrification on the way. And you know where there's gentrification, there's purging, these days.' Mary wasn't bothering to whisper and about a third of the diners were listening in. Their glances bounced between her and the sharks with increasing vigour.

'What are you going to do about it?'

'I've told them "No" in a sundry of ways at several volumes, but they seem to think they can do an unfriendly takeover, or some such. They claimed they want to keep the current staff on. I don't trust them as far as I can spit.'

Then their food was ready, and Adam and I took plate after plate over to them, Mary still standing guard by the swing door. I wanted to drop the moussaka in the lap of the one who'd ordered it, but I didn't.

We re-joined our boss, watching as they shared and picked their way through the food. The American ate one handed while with the other he moved his mock-up of our dining hall around. Betty, who brought her bairn in twice a week for a thin lunch of cottage cheese and tuna, took to sobbing.

All the while, I squeezed the flower in my pocket and thought how it *might* have brought luck today. Did it bring these three, instead?

Then, a new guest came through the front door. He went to stand behind the three men. I noticed that, despite the still bucketing weather outside, his coat was dry, no droplets clinging to his shaggy hair. A moment later, another person came in and stood beside the first. The room began to fill. More people came, through the front and also, through the swing door, one by one. They glided in, dressed in all sorts of styles that, let's face it, today could be today's. I recognised some as people I'd served years ago then lost track of, but there were others I'd never set eyes on before. They filed in, bringing with them a coolness that resembled the feeling in my glacial stomach. Each one headed straight to that central table, crowding round it until they were four and five deep, congregating around the three interlopers. The sharks.

Slowly, the conversation of the three men began to falter. The toff stopped talking, reaching to his buttoned-up neck to run a finger under his collar. How could he be hot with the sudden drop in the temperature? The other two twitched as if they had both been pinched at once. A pair of young boys covered their mouths in silent laughter and took a step back, the air flickering around them. The sharks immediately returned to their discussion.

I couldn't believe they didn't notice the crowd around them.

The rest of the diners and staff were no more clueful. The guests had gone back to their meals and their chats, to reading and scrolling their mobiles. Adam stood stolid, hands crossed in front of him like an old-fashioned cinema usher waiting for intermission. He was ready for action, but he didn't see what I saw. Raoul was in the kitchen, grill-cleaning noises issuing forth.

Only Mary seemed to be enjoying the spectacle. Her eyebrows were high with surprise, but the corners of her mouth were turning up and her eyes began to dance. I tested the waters, in case I was mistaken, 'Mary?'

'Do you see them, Daph?'

'Aye.'

As we spoke, the crowding of the room reached seemingly explosive proportions, like if one more soul set foot between the walls, they'd bulge outwards, then shatter, and we'd get washed away in the autumn downpour.

The sharks continued to talk and to stick food in their gobs, despite their complexions draining away. The figures around them pressed closer and closer and an old manny swung his umbrella up from his side. Holding it like a pool cue—though how he had room to manoeuvre at all I couldn't understand—he prodded each of the men a sharp shunt in their ribs.

Mary whispered, 'Blimey! I never thought they had it in them.'

I held tight to the flower as it all came clear. My boss had been talking with these shades!

Now, the men sat up ram-rod straight and looked over their shoulders. Still blind to the host of people in the room, they seemed to forget the prodding of moments before, relaxed, and made to return to their discussion, but just then, the figures converged on them. At that moment, you could see that the sharks felt the pressure of so many souls. There was a gasp from the Yank, then they were raised up: squeezed and lifted and carried, their limbs gyrating in slow-motion that made them look as if they were swimming towards the outside door. Their belongings and overcoats tumbled along with them.

By now the diners were staring at the sight of the three men being propelled out of the room. It must have appeared to them that they were in a flow of oil. Some watched, open mouthed, while others bent their heads back to their plates, not wanting to see. A small cheer came from the direction of Betty.

I was enthralled by the sight of the myriad of figures, all of them almost not there. Translucent, layer upon layer of images like someone had placed celluloid films of people on top of each other and shone a light through them. Or the way autumn leaves get when, spread out across the pavement, the weather has battered them to ghosts of themselves, all the colours of the season bleeding into each other.

When they were gone, the sharks I mean, it was as if the room breathed a sigh of relief. The diners let their shoulders drop, began talking in hushed tones, chewed their food again instead of toying with it. The translucent people stood for a moment longer enjoying the old room, then looked over at Mary and nodded to her. Then, they began to drift, some past us into the back room again, some out to the street, others through the wall. I thought I saw catwalk girl, her ruined coat and her dishevelled hair immaculate.

In no time, they were gone. Adam cleared the used plates off the vacated table, wiped it down. I stood, hands limp, feeling a surge of pride in our place. 'Do you think they'll come back?'

'No, not that lot. If they weren't scared out of their shorts, there's something seriously wrong with 'em.' Any signs Mary had shown of being past it were gone now. I realised, of course, with shame, that the indications had all been in my head. I admonished myself, *Prejudiced much?* I'd been hinging my thoughts on a number, but now, I was willing to bet on Mary for another ten years, at least. In my pocket, I turned the flower the catwalk girl had left for me.

Then Mary said, 'I'm thinking of taking it a little easier around here. What do you say, Daphne, to finally getting to manage this place?'

Rhoda is an omniwriter (novels, short stories, poetry, essays, etc) living in Dundee, who whatever her body is doing in what we call real life, spends most of her days with wee stories and characters circling round her mind. She also walks a lot with a miniature schnauzer called Islay May.

Words Written in Water

Deborah L. Davitt

The first time Lenore saw the words written in the water, she was just ten. She sat beside her father on the riverbank, his company a rare and sought-after privilege, solemnly holding her fishing pole and being *quiet*. Papa said too much talking scared the fish away.

It'd taken her till she was thirty to suspect that perhaps it wasn't just the fish that didn't like chattering.

But on that golden afternoon, waiting for the swift-darting shadows under the water to take an experimental nibble on a baited hook, she saw words rising up from where the fish dwelled. Words that seemed like mighty lunkers that she'd never catch. They burned as brightly as the sunlight reflecting from the stillness of the shallows, and they read, *A farewell wreath floats.*

She tugged her father's elbow, to his irritation, pointing at the words, breath tight in her chest. Lenore knew she was supposed to be *quiet*, so she could scarcely form words of her own.

But Papa didn't see the words. "If you can't hush, I guess we're going home," he told her, frowning. And she wept, silently, all the way back to the house, kicking at the dirt of the road with her bare feet.

She tried to tell Mama about the words. And Mama listened, frowning and troubled. "It might have been a message from a river spirit," Mama said.

"Papa says spirits aren't real. He says the mills being built, the dam, those are real." Lenore sniffled. "A farewell wreath sounds bad."

Mama hugged her. "Might not be. Just . . . don't go back to the river for a good while, all right? Might have been a warning against drowning."

"That's fine. I don't want to go back. I want to go to other countries! Like India, maybe."

Mama didn't comment on a child's dreams.

Lenore had almost forgotten the words—pushed them beneath the surface of her mind, where they lurked, like dark fish—until seven years later, when the rains came, heavy and fierce. They broke the new dam, flooding the village. And her father died, swept away by the floodwaters while trying to help old Mrs. Curry escape her house.

They laid a wreath for him on a rock along the riverside after the waters receded. Lenore touched the sand-abraded surface. "I sat here with him, fishing," she told her mother softly.

But her mother was in no place to hear the words, lost in a world of her own grief.

The second time Lenore saw the words written in the water, she stood on the new stone bridge, newly-wed, hand-in-hand with her husband, Elliot. They couldn't afford a carriage, so they'd walked from the church after the ceremony. And with sundown staining the leaden waters a dull red, she looked over the edge, and saw words rippling there once more: *on the river of regret.*

"Let's move away from here," Lenore blurted to Elliot. "I hate this place. It killed my father."

Elliot gave her a patient look, squeezing her hand. "The flood hit my family, too. I understand. But . . ." he gestured at the big textile mills looming on the horizon, "this is where we both work, Lenore. How are we *supposed* to move anywhere else?"

Words tangled up in her throat. How could she convey that the river *spoke* to her? Told her that she'd regret living here? That it would take more lives from her than just her father's? Or perhaps, this time, it was telling her that she'd regret working for the mills?

It took her two years to realize that the *regret* she'd feel was for marrying Elliot. She hadn't known him as a child. His family had moved to the village not long before her father's death. The rages, the drinking—those didn't start till he lost his job at the mill, while she'd managed to cling to shift work. And so he sat at the pub, drinking her earnings and shouting at her for not having dinner ready the moment she came home from her twelve-hour shift at the water-driven looms.

She gritted her teeth. Talked a shift-manager into taking Elliot back into the factory. Hoped that somehow, honest employment and hours spent in useful toil would somehow turn him back into the man she'd married.

For a while it almost seemed to work.

Then another drunken argument. "How'd you get Tomlinson to give you a raise?"

"I thought you'd be *happy*. We can *move* out—away from the river—"

"Did you fuck him? Is that how?"

"No! Why would you *say* something like that?"

He forced her out of their house by the riverside, bruising her wrists with his clenched hands—and threw her to the rounded stones on the bank. In the moonlight, she caught the words in the ripples in a flash as he fumbled for one of the rocks: *shores stained with sorrows.*

The words were blood-red.

She rolled to the side as he brought the rock down at her head, still screaming at her, and she frantically kicked at the backs of his knees.

It wouldn't have worked, the coroner agreed, if he hadn't been so drunk and so off-balance. As it was, he fell into the river and hit his head on the stones there, and Lenore sat there, shaking and bruised, waiting for him to come back up, spitting and raging.

The police wanted to call it manslaughter. Kept asking, "Why didn't you pull him out? Call a neighbor for help? Did you want him to die?"

"I was too scared," she whispered. "He... didn't like the neighbors to know when he'd gotten upset."

But there was a whisper at the back of her mind that said, *Maybe you <u>did</u> want him to die. Just a little. Or maybe you thought the river would just . . . take care of it.*

Lenore hadn't known she was pregnant. And as she wore widow's black, though she hardly mourned, her body swelled with new life. But her daughter didn't look much like Elliot, and so she didn't *think* she'd regret bearing the girl. But now, it seemed even harder to escape the river and the village. She couldn't just quit her job at the mill and move elsewhere. She had little Mina to think of, after all. She liked the name she'd given the girl, at least— it meant *fish*, in the language of a country she'd never get to visit.

Years turned into decades, and Lenore had almost forgotten once again that the river had ever spoken to her. Carriages became automobiles, but she still worked at the mills, long into the night, so that Mina might have a better life than she'd had. In fact, she managed to send her off to *college*, something no one else in town had ever done. "Don't make me regret this," she told Mina sternly as she handed her daughter into the jalopy that would take her and her luggage to the distant city where the school stood.

"I won't," Mina assured her, laughing. "Thank you, Mama!"

A quick, distracted kiss on her cheek, and then Mina was gone. Her presence had warped the shape of Lenore's life, displacing so many other things, like a stone thrown into water, that Lenore wasn't really sure now who she was. Certainly not the girl who'd married Elliot. Nor the woman who'd feared to save him. Not even the girl who'd baited worms and fished beside her father on the river banks.

Watching the automobile putter off, Lenore stood on the weathered stone of the old bridge, looking down at the river's waters, stained with the filth of the mills. To her surprise, she could see words there again—not threatening this time. *As petals drift downstream, from past into the future…*

She sighed. "I think you only gave me part of the message. But I think I get the gist. Time passes. God, how it does."

She didn't tell Mina about the words until Mina came home with a medical degree. Lenore's hands ached with arthritis these days, and the long days at the mill took more and more out of her. "What do you mean, there were words in the water?" Mina demanded.

So she told her the whole story. "Stress," Mina determined, in her wholly rational way.

"I don't think so, dear. The words were there, even before I knew they meant something. Interlaced into the very molecules, perhaps."

"Tell me you don't think Grandma's fantasy about *river spirits*, hah, carries any water."

Lenore decided not to talk more with Mina about it. "I don't think it has to do with a spirit," she admitted. "I think it has to do with *time*. How it's... all one piece."

Mina gave her the look that the college-educated often give those who haven't been similarly blessed, and started talking about gravity and space and time. Lenore let the words flow over her like water. They were probably good words. Words that hadn't been assembled in those configurations when she'd been a girl. But they weren't *her* words, or the words of the river.

The last time she saw the words, Lenore was teaching her grandson how to write by tracing letters in the smooth sand on the far bank of the river. The textile mills stood, rusting, empty hulks in the distance, and the waters once again ran clear, tamed by a concrete dam upstream.

On a whim, she wrote each line that the river had once whispered to her.

A farewell wreath floats
on the river of regret;
petals drift downstream
from past into the future

"What does all that mean, Grandma?" the boy asked.

Lenore smiled, and wrote a final line: *time has the meaning you give.* "I'll tell you later," she whispered, and watched as the water rose, rippling, and dissolved every word.

Deborah L. Davitt *was raised in Nevada, but currently lives in Houston, Texas with her husband and son. Her award-winning poetry and prose has appeared in over seventy journals, including F&SF, Asimov's, Analog, and Lightspeed. For more about her work, including her Elgin-placing poetry collections, Bounded by Eternity and From Voyages Unreturning, see www.deborahldavitt.com.*

No Such Thing as Monsters

DJ Cockburn

It was Aunt Laura who cracked first.

When Jilly walked into the living room with Freddy the Teddy in her hand, Aunt Laura was in the armchair while Mum and Dad were on the sofa. They were watching telly together and didn't look as unhappy as they had for most of the last three days. Jilly hoped that meant they might start looking happy in another three days.

Dad was the first to see Jilly. He got off the sofa and came to her. "What's the matter, precious?'"

"Can't sleep," said Jilly.

"Oh dear." Daddy picked her up. "Why not?"

"Just can't."

"Is it that naughty monster under the bed?" asked Dad. "Shall I go and tell him off?"

Jilly was six years old which was far too old to believe in monsters under beds. She was about to tell Dad not to be silly but Aunt Laura spoke first.

"Those who speak with certainty have assured us that monsters no longer hide under beds," she said. "We are duly informed that they all crawled out last week and now they're rampaging around on our once-but-no-longer safe streets."

Aunt Laura waved at the window, indicating the night beyond the closed curtains where pure darkness had replaced the streetlight glow on the first night Aunt Laura had stayed with them.

Mum made the face that Jilly knew meant 'be quiet' but Aunt Laura had only come to stay three days ago and hadn't learned mum's faces yet.

"It's true," said Aunt Laura. "That's what the government says and the government never lies to us, do they?"

Dad held Jilly a little closer. "Yes, well, they won't hurt us as long as we stay at home so there's nothing to worry about."

"And the scientists. They're telling us the monsters are out there as well," said Aunt Laura. "Scientists always know best. Just like with thalidomide and Fukushima. So we can all sleep safe in our beds as long as we're good boys and girls and leave the streets to the monsters."

Jilly felt Dad's arm tighten around her. She wasn't sure what it meant but it made her feel a lot less safe than when he picked her up. At the same time, it stopped her from asking him to put her down.

"Jilly's been a very good girl and she still can't sleep so perhaps we can. Change. The. Damn. Record," said Dad.

Mum's face was now saying, 'be quiet right now'. Jilly didn't like looking at that face so she turned away and saw Kim was standing in the living room doorway. It was the first time Kim had left her bedroom since lunch. Since she turned fourteen and started wearing black eye shadow, Kim often appeared in doorways where she stood in silence, neither entering one room nor leaving another.

"All right. Record changed," said Aunt Laura.

"Thank you." Dad untightened a little.

"There is absolutely no doubt at all that the streets outside are infested with monstrously monstrous monsters," said Aunt Laura.

"Will you *give it a rest*?" Mum's voice blasted Aunt Laura's aside like the big bad wolf blowing down the little pig's house of sticks. "Three days we've listened to your banging on. We asked you to stay with us because we thought it might be tough for you on your own but all you do is drive us round the bend with your non-stop sarcasm."

If Jilly had warned Aunt Laura about Mum's 'be quiet' face, Aunt Laura would have known to be quiet but Jilly hadn't said anything, which made it partly Jilly's fault that Mum had lost her temper. Jilly put her mouth close to Dad's ear and said, "sorry," but he probably didn't hear because Mum's lost-temper voice was so loud.

When Mum was like this, the only thing to do was concentrate very hard on something and wait for her to run out of words. Jilly pulled Freddy in front of her so she could peek between his ears and concentrate on Kim's frown.

The week before the school closed, Miss Schofield had shown Jilly's class how to put things in order by how big or how heavy they were. When she came home that day, Jilly realised she could put Kim's frowns in order from one to five. When she first saw Kim in the doorway, she'd been frowning a three but now it had deepened all the way to five.

Mum's voice fell silent. The thing to do now was to keep very still and very quiet until Mum said something in a less angry tone of voice.

Aunt Laura didn't know that. "You're right of course. The media agree with the scientists and the government and everybody knows the *Daily Mail* always tells the truth."

Mum's face changed from red to white and her eyes opened wider than Jilly had ever seen them. Jilly had only seen that face once, when Kim and her friend drank Mum and Dad's bottle of wine. She hadn't given that face a name because she hoped she'd never see it again.

Aunt Laura raised both hands as if she thought Mum was turning into one of the monsters and was about to attack her.

Got it, thought Jilly, *Mum's monster face.*

"OK, I'm sorry," said Aunt Laura, who badly needed someone to tell her when to stop saying anything. "And I'm grateful that you asked me to stay with you. Really I am. I'm not used to being surrounded by people all the time. I'm used to having a lot more time on my own."

"I can see why," said Kim.

Aunt Laura and Mum's heads rotated to look at her. Jilly held her breath and buried her face in Freddy. Kim rarely spoke at all and she certainly knew better than to speak when Mum had lost her temper.

The sound that Mum filled the room with surprised Jilly so much that it took her a moment to realise that Mum was not yelling but laughing. Jilly dared to look and saw Mum's face had changed back to red, but this time it was a happy red. Mum was laughing so hard that she was half lying on the sofa where Dad had been sitting.

Jilly couldn't understand what was so funny. Aunt Laura didn't look like she understood either. She wasn't smiling as she watched Mum.

Aunt Laura's mouth turned into a hard line and she glared at Kim. "That was uncalled for."

Kim shrugged.

"We're all making an effort to get along," said Aunt Laura. "Being snippy doesn't help and take my word for it, young lady, that sort of comment might sound clever in your head but it doesn't sound half as clever when you say it aloud."

Kim said, "OK, boomer."

Mum had been sitting up, but she burst out laughing and fell flat on the sofa again.

Dad said, "Can we all take this down a couple of-"

"Boomer?" Aunt Laura didn't let him finish. "*Boomer*? I'm barely fifty! Which is still thirty-five years more experience of life than you. And if there's one thing I've learned in that time, it's to be very, very sceptical of politicians, journalists, scientists and anyone else who tells me to stay off the streets for my own good."

Jilly had never seen Kim frown past a five before. She was going to have to start grading out of ten because Kim's frown had dropped to at least a seven and was still sinking.

"I don't care if they're talking about monsters under the bed or monsters on the streets. Who's ever seen a single one of them?" Aunt Laura glared around the room like Miss Schofield telling the whole class off for making too much noise. "I'll tell you who. No one. Not one person has seen a monster because there's no such thing as monsters. Don't look at me as if you don't believe me. I'll show you."

Aunt Laura leapt out of the chair and marched for the front door.

"Hold on a minute." Dad was following her, still carrying Jilly, but Aunt Laura took no notice. She flung open the front door and strode into the night.

"There you are." Aunt Laura's voice came from the darkness. "Not a monster to be seen."

"Laura, come back inside," said Dad. "And keep your voice down. They'll hear you."

Jilly peered through the open door but she couldn't see Aunt Laura. All she could see was darkness.

"Laura." Dad raised his voice, making Jilly flinch away from him. "You've made your point. Come back inside."

No answer came from the night.

"*Laura.*"

Nobody spoke. Nobody answered.

Dad put Jilly down. "Stay there, precious."

He stepped in front of her, leaned forward and pushed the front door closed with his fingertips.

DJ Cockburn funded his unfortunate writing habit through medical research on various parts of the African continent and drinking a lot of coffee. Earlier phases of his life have included teaching unfortunate children and experimenting on unfortunate fish.

In between a steady drizzle of rejections, he's seen a few stories in venues including Apex, Interzone and Gardner Dozois's Year's Best Science Fiction for 2014, and he won the 2014 James White Award.

His website is at http://cockburndj.wordpress.com/ and is on Bluesky as @djcockburn.bsky.social.

Xenogamy

Rob Gillham

"You, Jerome Faulkes, are a deviant," says my interrogator.

The featureless room is washed in cold, unforgiving light from the overhead strip bulb, rendering everything in a mortuary pallor. The vibration of Caerfort's distant, antediluvian engines is a reassuring presence. Wherever it is they've brought me, we haven't left the station.

The Quaestor makes careful notes in a leather-bound folio with a fountain pen. "When I say that," she says, not looking up, "I mean you are a petty criminal—a known distributor of pornographic and dissident works. I care little about such things. My purpose is to determine whether you are also an enemy of the Commonwealth."

She's a striking woman—late-twenties, dark-skinned and handsome, dressed in a sober charcoal suit. The eyes that stare at me are gold and incongruous—obvious upgrades. I appreciate the vulgar artifice in their artificiality. They render an otherwise likeable, youthful face remote and unknowable.

She looks up and—seeing my attention—smiles before making further notes.

I'm almost admiring the theatricality of the moment before I check myself. Quaestor Laurenz Diawara is astute. She will have been recruited from one of Earth's finest schools, before being subjected to years of training and indoctrination. Every facet of this performance, every tic and gesture will have been carefully judged, weighted, practised, and honed to maximise its impact on an interview subject.

I maintain a brittle smile just long enough that she sees it. After all, I have an image to maintain. I am a deviant, and in my long and nefarious career, I have been threatened by experts.

All my bravado doesn't alter the fact that if Diawara decides I'm guilty, it is the end. People audited by the Quaestors go away and do not come back.

She replaces the pen lid and delicately places it on the table, exactly parallel to the folio. "Now, Jerome Faulkes, let us begin."

Finding my emporium is something of a dark art. It's not the sort of establishment where passers-by drop in to browse. Viewings are possible only by prior appointment—or prior knowledge— and possession of either implies I want you to find me. If I don't wish to entertain them, a would-be visitor might search for me for years without success. The shop's featureless black door sits in a corridor indistinguishable from the hundreds riddling every level of Rat 2. Across all five wings of Caerfort's panoptical structure, anonymous entrances just like it must number in the thousands.

As it is, I've no appointments today. I sit in an armchair with the strains of Bach echoing through the towering book stacks, deeply immersed in Boris Pasternak's Russian translation of Goethe's *Faust*. The book is a 1953 edition with illustrations by A. Goncharov: not a deviant text as such, but certainly problematic. It is beautiful.

Prudence descends headfirst from the darkness of the stacks overhead, scuttling down bookshelves like a lizard. "Someone is coming," she hisses.

"Then get off the wall, you silly girl," — I put the book down — "and zip your top up. This isn't a bawdy house."

She gets within twenty metres of the floor and releases her grip on the wall, turning a neat backflip and landing on her feet like a gymnast. She glares at me with huge green eyes and pulls the zip of her dark red jumpsuit up to the neck. "Satisfied?"

I take her head in both hands and place a kiss on the alabaster skin of her forehead, just below the line of dark hair pulled back in a severe ponytail. "Eminently—now you are presentable. I don't want people saying my niece is a strumpet."

She scowls at me. "I'm not your niece—and a good thing too, considering the things you like to do to me."

I wag a finger. "Be a good girl, Prudence."

The buzzer sounds. I check the external camera. "The estimable Sergeant Shamon."

Prudence expels a disgusted breath. "He thinks about impregnating me. I can smell the pheromones when he stares at me like a hungry dog. I'm going back up till he's gone."

She squats, then propels herself upwards, grabbing a lighting rail that runs across the width of the shop. She scales the shelves noiselessly and within seconds is consumed by the gloom of their heights.

The space my shop occupies is the height of two of Caerfort's unlovely, Bauhaus-efficient units. I procured the one above mine and removed the interconnecting floor years ago. Prudence prefers to observe my dealings from the lightless apogee of this additional elevation rather than interact with people herself. I've never been able to determine if this is due to innate awkwardness combined with unnatural agility, or some deeper-rooted instinct that, if real, seems more arachnid than human.

I press the entrance control and the half-metre-thick door opens with a sigh of released air. Sergeant Joachim Shamon grins at me as he enters. The dapper militiaman who arrived on Caerfort some twenty years ago has long since gone to seed, his appearance growing increasingly piratical as he careers into late-middle age. "Jerome Faulkes, you old sinner."

He is unshaven, with curly hair hanging long around his ears. His grey uniform is a harlequinade of patchwork additions and sits taut around his burgeoning midriff. He places his hands on his hips and glances around the towering bookshelves. "Where's that delightful wildcat you keep around here?"

"Prudence is out."

Shamon pouts. "Shame." He places a black bundle on the counter and takes a stool without being asked. "Busy time. A merchantman just came in—the *Rozkol*. She's been five years out on the Eastern frontier. Her arrival caused a helluva fuss. She's berthed in Rat 1 while the auditors go through her with a fine-tooth comb—crew, cargo, ship's log, you name it." He pauses. "Got anything to drink around here?"

I retrieve a bottle of scotch and two tumblers from behind the counter and pour a measure into each glass. "Rat 1? The captain must be well-connected."

Rat 1 is the administrative headquarters of Caerfort and the nearest thing to a state of law and order the station offers. It's also exclusive. Much of my clientele lives there, and passage from the other parts of the station is strictly controlled through the panoptical gate. Most visiting ships get berthed in the lower rats where their crew and passengers can do as they please without lowering the tone.

Shamon takes the proffered tumbler. He sips and winces. "These guys aren't high-fliers. The ship's just come back from the Eastern frontier. That's triggered a priority investigation by the auditors. You know there's alien junk from the archaeological digs openly on sale out there—art, tech, plants, anything goes."

I know—just as I know why Shamon's here. The Sergeant of the Watch is as corrupt as Caerfort's artificial day is long. "Let me guess—the *Rozkol*'s being taken apart rivet by rivet, and somebody onboard has something they'd rather the auditors didn't find." I can't help glancing at the black bundle on the counter. I don't merely want to know what's in it now—I need to know.

Shamon grins. "Let's just say I've been commissioned to act as agent for a party who wants the sale of a certain objet d'art expedited without any tiresome import controls." He nods. "Take a look."

I force myself not to grab at the black cloth bag. Instead, I gently pull it across the counter towards me. I tease apart the drawstrings and take out a rectangular cuboid about the size of my palm. It's constructed of a hard, dark material like ebony. Only, it's not wood at all. The surface is covered in raised, similarly shaped symbols which overlap like fish scales. I run a finger over them. The symbols have a certain three-dimensional quality—some are raised further from the body of the cube than others, some curling up at the edges while others lie flat. I'd be willing to bet each symbol is unique. My heartbeat is a reverberating, thudding bass drum. "This box alone is an item of considerable value." I glance up at Shamon. "It is a box, I take it?"

His smile has withered to a tight line. "The catch is on the side."

My thumb finds some give in one of the scales. I depress it and the shape unfolds to reveal its contents.

Alien. How carelessly we throw that word around. To gaze upon something crafted by another species is to be reminded precisely what the term entails: exotic, opposed, incompatible.

I am almost overcome by the wave of dissonance evoked by the object within. Its sheer otherness—the beauty of it—is soul-numbing. It is the most aberrant, appalling thing I have ever seen. It is quite, quite wonderful.

I apply the smallest pressure to the sides of the box. It folds itself back into its original shape, enclosing the thing within. "Is it biological matter?" My voice is a hoarse croak. The contents of this box would cost a king's ransom. I don't care. I crave it. I would call Prudence down and have her rip Shamon to shreds right now if I thought that was the only way to secure this prize.

Shamon knocks back the contents of his tumbler as if he's drinking rotgut in a Rat 5 bordello and not seventy-year-old Glenfiddich. "The owner requested a trustworthy broker to hold that thing securely until a buyer could be found. Naturally, I thought of you."

Yes, he would have. Shamon must suspect I have a quantum-locked vault—not that I'd ever admit to such a thing. Quantum vaults occupy that grey area between problematic and officially deviant technology. I'm certain they're alien in origin—just as I suspect the only reason they're not explicitly prohibited is because the rich and powerful find them so incredibly useful.

I'm still cupping the little black cuboid in both hands as though it's a holy relic. My throat is dry and I swallow spit. "The party who safeguards the item would presumably have first refusal to purchase it?"

Shamon shrugs. "It can't hurt. I told them you're trustworthy and discreet, and have the means to keep it tucked away from prying eyes. For what it's worth, I think they were originally planning to find a buyer on Earth. Now the auditors are sniffing around, I guess they'd prefer a quick sale here to get it off their hands."

I look at the object sitting in my palm. It is—very nearly—the most inherently wrong thing I have ever seen. I want it so badly, the need is a gnawing sensation in my gut.

Quaestor Diawara regards me with implacable patience. For something to do, I count the seconds. One minute and eight seconds later, she says, "You like music, Jerome."

I say nothing. She smiles and inclines her head slightly. "When we raided your premises, there was music playing—Bach's Brandenburg Concerto Number Four. Very old. Very unusual."

"Bach isn't problematic music." I curse inwardly. There was no need to respond.

Her smile broadens. "And yet—it is obscure in the extreme, hard to find. Your tastes run to such things, don't they? Unusual, rare, secret things."

I still the answer on my lips. These are merely opening shots across the bows, precursors to the real questions. I won't condemn myself out of hand like the Earthbound fodder I imagine Quaestor Diawara has cut her teeth on—terrified bureaucrats caught with mildly pornographic pictures bought to spice up bland existences lived in pattern-based homes with their carefully unexceptional wardrobes and art generated to strictly approved parameters.

Diawara reaches into a case on the floor by her seat and retrieves a small pile of books and magazines which she places on the table between us.

"Animal Farm, Playboy Magazine, Mein Kampf, Huckleberry Finn, Bitches In Heat Volume Two, Lolita, The Complete Predictions of Nostradamus, Slaughterhouse-Five." She sweeps a hand over the pile. "All these publications are officially classified somewhere on the scale between problematic and class C deviancy."

This is not a question either.

She wrinkles her nose. "Low-grade smut and the works of long-dead lunatics and perverts." She taps the pile with her index finger. "Oh, yes—*Faust*, in the old Russian language. You can read it, Jerome?"

I suppress a shudder as her fingernail leaves small indents on the priceless hardback cover. "A little slowly, but yes."

"How very unconventional." The warmth of the Quaestor's smile chafes. I must be thirty years older than her. Her assumed persona—indulgent headteacher dealing with an intelligent but errant schoolchild—feels inappropriate. The lack of forethought revealed by her approach is almost insulting.

Is she even a full quaestor? If so, she can't have been one for very long. Perhaps Laurenz Diawara has overreached herself.

"Johann Faustus, Jerome Faulkes," she says as if the thought has only just occurred to her. "Interesting coincidence. I wonder whether you see yourself in Doctor Faustus—a man in touch with dark forces. Have you made a deal with the Devil, Jerome?" The merest hint of a smile dances around the edges of her mouth.

I meet her expression with a blank stare. "No, I do not imagine myself to be in communion with dark forces."

"Oh, but that's not true, Jerome." She leans forward. "That's not true at all, is it?"

Laurenz Diawara is the first person I have ever met who can openly admit to knowledge of *Faust*'s contents. The thought causes me to shiver. I want to ask her if she has read it all the way through, what she thought of it.

Most of my clientele come to me purely for the transgressive thrill of owning books. Prudence has even less interest in reading, being incapable of understanding why people tell one another stories that are essentially untrue.

Prudence drops silently to the floor. Shamon has departed. The drawstring bag remains on the counter. I've been staring at it for over ten minutes.

She sniffs, nostrils flaring as she peers at the black bundle. "What is it? It stinks."

"You heard Shamon." I pat the bag. "We've been given it for safekeeping."

Her thick eyebrows furrow, causing small creases to appear in the otherwise smooth skin around her forehead and eyes. "Is it alien?"

"What makes you say that?" I fight to keep my tone ambivalent. After all, if anyone could intuit the object's provenance, it should be her.

"Can't you smell it?"

"I lack your superior senses." I gesture around the book stacks. "I smell nothing but the musty wisdom of the ancients."

Prudence bares her teeth in an expression that is so canine I almost expect her to growl. "It's vile. I hate it." She places both hands on my arm. "Get rid of it. Please, Uncle."

"You only call me that when you want something." I laugh and pat her on the leg. "And I can't get rid of it. It must be kept safe."

"Shamon wants it kept…in the vault?"

I frown. "Yes. He damn near said as much too." Shamon has never been interested in such details before. It's always been sufficient for him that the business he puts my way commands a healthy finder's fee. *See no evil, speak no evil* is the deviant's maxim—pass it on, then forget about it. "You'll have to put up with it for a little while yet."

Her eyebrows arch. "Please, no. It's nasty."

"Don't be so silly." Prudence's tendency to reach for a child's vocabulary when excised is one of her less charming attributes.

She sticks out her lower lip and rests her head on my shoulder. "Is it dangerous to have? I don't want anything to happen to you."

I push her away gently. "Very loyal of you, but don't sulk. You aren't pretty when you pout."

Prudence is, to all intents and purposes, in her early twenties, but she's never learnt to mask her feelings. And I lied—she is very pretty when she pouts.

Her visceral dislike of my prize has made me irritable. For a brief instant, I consider pushing the matter further, making her cry, just to see tears run down her beautiful face. Something about that thought produces a delicious, bittersweet tug at my heart which is almost too painful to bear. I dismiss the idea. There is no time for self-indulgence. The artefact is too valuable, too important—it must be secured without delay.

I tap the black bag. "Nothing happens to this, do you understand? It's very important. I could be in some danger if it were discovered. You don't want that, do you?"

"No." Her voice is small and tremulous.

I get up and move towards the back room. At the door, I glance back. Prudence still stands by my vacated stool, clenching and unclenching her hands, her expression that of a lost little girl.

By design, Prudence will instantly kill anyone she perceives as a danger to me. Yet, for all her assured lethality, when faced with a more intangible threat, she can only fret. That, I suppose, is my fault. When you can detect the tell-tale biology of a lie, how can you ever learn the necessity of half-truths and compromise?

Anywhere but the half-lit world of Caerfort, my ward's talents and shortcomings would attract unwanted scrutiny. And if anyone ever learnt precisely what she was, the auditors would be the least of my problems.

"You're an educated man, Jerome." Diawara's tone is conversational. "Tell me, why are the different wings of this station called rats?" She half-smiles. "No one's been able to tell me."

"The station is a rat king," I say.

She frowns in mock ignorance.

"When rats become too numerous for the space they occupy, their tails can become hopelessly entangled," I say. "Rats knotted together like this will surrender their individual instincts and become a single entity, each facing outward, completely dependent on the others for defence and survival. Someone with a poor sense of humour decided the station resembled five rats all joined at the tail."

Diawara nods. She knew this, of course. "Well, this 'rat king' is a cause of increasing concern for the Office of the Quaestor General. Caerfort may be an important crossroads for inter-system trade, but it's also self-serving, a law unto itself." She gestures around herself. "The administration here pays lip service to the Commonwealth and the rule of law, but it's compromised. Officials openly deal with criminal elements. Their greed creates a conflict of interest."

"Greed?"

She nods as if taking me seriously. "The administrators of this station didn't get rich from berth fees. We estimate twelve per cent of all Earth-bound cargo passing through Caerfort is disposed of on the shadow market." She grimaces. "And of course, such activity encourages more insidious kinds of criminal trade" — she fixes me with those expressionless gold eyes — "your kind of trade, Jerome."

How long is this game to continue—Diawara feigning friendliness and honest enquiry while I counter with wide-eyed innocence? There's no time limit to the potential length of my detention.

"What does the term 'xenogamy' mean to you?" The sharpness of her tone brings me up short.

"Something to do with crops?" Of course, I know what it means.

She reopens the leather-bound folio and begins to flip through the pages. "Historically, it was a term describing the transplantation of exotic pollen to another plant. More recently, it has come to refer to the contamination of a world's ecosystem by alien flora and fauna." She stops leafing and places a finger on the open page. "Three inhabited worlds in Kepler-11 are currently quarantined due to an infestation of a seaweed-like, non-CO_2-producing alien plant that kills all Earth crops introduced by the colonists."

She turns a page. "The Rubin observation station in Gliese 180 has been in lockdown for three years, due to contamination by an invasive alien bacteria that sterilised seventy-eight per cent of the station's population, but not before some station crew fled to nearby worlds. We're monitoring all three of the system's inhabited planets for any signs of outbreak. A naval blockade of the entire system remains a very real possibility."

"I am aware of the prohibitions on trade in alien—"

"Shut up, Faulkes." Her voice is hard, all pretence of amity gone. "You will listen to me. My priority is to prevent alien contamination at all costs. I do not care that you peddle trash perpetuating the political, religious, sexual, and racial obsessions that dogged humanity's past. Your so-called deviancy is nothing but the impulse of a child that wants something simply because it is forbidden." Her speech slows, the tone calm and steady. "Nonetheless, the items from your shop provide me with all the pretext I need to send you to a labour colony."

My pulse quickens, but I can't resist a jibe. "Yet, by your admission, my alleged activities are beneath your notice, Laurenz."

"That's *Quaestor Diawara* to you, Faulkes." Her voice is calm, but her eyebrows furrow into a furious scowl. "Do you imagine you can talk down to me with impunity? Perhaps your immersion in antiquated dogma has confused you."

She is a full quaestor then. Yet, it appears my childish barb landed. Can Diawara really be driven to anger by something as inconsequential as being cheeked by a minor deviant?

Of course not. Have a care, Faulkes.

Quaestor Diawara sighs. She places the fingertips of both hands together to form a peak. "Misogyny is such an anachronistic form of deviancy that trainee quaestors today are taught it's harmless, a once-virulent disease we inoculated humanity against long ago." She stares at me over her steepled fingers and gives me a thin, wintry smile. "Understand this, Jerome—your perverse scholarship and that superior, old-world manner may cow and awe the inhabitants of this sewer, but they make no impression on me. I hold absolute power over you. Nothing you can say or do can alter that."

She holds my gaze for a moment. A thousand retorts rush through my mind and die stillborn on my lips.

Diawara gives a tiny nod. "Now we understand one another, let us proceed." Her voice is steady and controlled. "Each day, ships from the Eastern fringe arrive here carrying crew and passengers with proscribed alien artefacts. They disembark, ask around—a quiet word in the right ear leads to other conversations, and inevitably, to you." She leans forward. "I already know that you fence alien artefacts, Jerome Faulkes. Your only hope is to make a full and immediate confession of this now."

So, finally, she has shown her hand. I shift in my seat. "I've nothing to say."

Her features slowly break into a broad smile. I'm immediately conscious of having made some horrible misstep. "Indeed," she says, "you've said so very little. Yet, I find it intriguing that, in all the time you've been here, you haven't even once asked after your niece."

Some cold mass comes free within me and plunges down my gullet like an iceberg calving from a collapsing glacier.

"A most curious young lady, your" — she checks her notebook — "Prudence. There are no entries for her in the station's birth records, nor any record of her arrival in any passenger manifest."

I dare not meet the Quaestor's golden gaze—not just now.

"Do you think she will fare well under interrogation? It must have occurred to you she is also a person of interest to us." She raises an eyebrow. "Nothing to say, Jerome?"

It doesn't require a quaestor's talents to identify there is something distinctly amiss about Prudence.

"Don't hurt her." I'm as shocked at the physical effort required to force the words from my mouth as I am at the hoarse whisper that emerges.

Diawara purses her lips. "Come now, Jerome. We don't hurt people—not often, anyway—not unless there's no other choice." She leans forward. "No more evasions. She's not your niece, is she?"

"No."

"A very pretty girl. Augmented, I imagine—even custom-grown?"

I look down. What is the smart thing to confess? Custom-grown human beings are illegal, yet this is nothing to the charge of handling alien materials. I'm trying to grasp Diawara's strategy and get a step ahead of her, but I can't hold a line of thought that doesn't dissolve into incoherent anguish at the thought of Prudence in a cell.

She lacks the awareness, and the self-control required to be unremarkable. She would lash out like a caged animal. Diawara must already know that Prudence is something more than human.

"Come on, Faulkes," Diawara snaps. "You don't have to spare my feelings. I'm a quaestor, not some virgin nun. Do you think you're the first ageing degenerate I've dealt with who owned a bespoke sex doll?"

"I suppose not." A tiny spark of hope kindles within me. Let Diawara believe this half-truth.

"If the girl's manufactured," says Diawara, "she'll have to be destroyed. You'll get twenty years in a labour colony. They're harsh environments. At your age, I don't think you'd last that long."

My hands ball into fists under the table. "Please, Quaestor Diawara. What do you want from me?"

Laurenz Diawara places both palms on the table, half-rising from her seat. "Everything. You will give me the contents of your quantum vault and everything else: the names of your clientele, the officials who aid you, the ships' captains you do business with. Everything."

It's so obvious, I want to laugh. I am not important, merely a means to an end. The Quaestor has her eyes set on a far greater prize. "You want all that, in return for what—my freedom?" I'm horrified to discover my eyes are wet with the first suggestion of tears. "What about Prudence?"

Diawara's artificial gaze has all the life and humanity of a stone effigy. There is no further pretence, no lightness—only contempt. "The girl might be permitted to live, but you shall never be free, Faulkes. From this moment onward, you are mine."

Her ugly gaze beholds me triumphantly and in this moment, I see Laurenz Diawara—not truly a person at all, but a bland, mass-produced simulacrum of intelligence—a thing convinced of its own righteousness, one that cares nothing for art, poetry or beauty, and values nothing except those qualities it admires in itself.

What is all my wickedness when set against such awful, implacable fanaticism?

My shop is being gutted. An ant-like procession of grey-uniformed auditorial staff carry out crates of confiscated stock to load onto the robotic cargo carrier blocking the thoroughfare outside.

The activity pauses to allow our party to enter. I am sandwiched between an advance party of Shamon and three of his militia, with Diawara and two more black-uniformed quaestors close behind me.

Shamon and his goons led us here via a quixotic route through abandoned units and derelict corridors, ducts, and tunnels. Diawara didn't want anyone to witness my humbling. If it became widely known I'd been arrested, my usefulness to her would be over.

I've caught Shamon studying me en route when he thinks no one else sees—attempting to gauge how broken I am, whether I've given him up to Diawara along with everything else. I haven't yet, but of course, I shall.

The plastic zip tie binding my wrists behind my back is cutting off the circulation. I twist my hands back and forth, hissing at the pain. Periodically, my contortions earn me a poke in the back with the point of a quaestor's baton. Both bindings and the prods have no practical purpose—the two uniformed quaestors could easily overpower me—they simply reinforce my new status.

Diawara walks into the centre of the shop, observing the activity surrounding her. The lower shelves are all but empty. Auditors scale the higher stacks with ladders. They've barely begun stripping these. The shelves beyond the lighting rig groan with items. I barely know what's up there in the highest, darkest places myself. I rely on Prudence for that.

Prudence. I screw my eyes shut and reopen them, trying to banish her captivity from my imagination. The quaestors will not be as gentle with her as they've been with me. To them, she is sub-human, non-existent.

"Attention. Stop what you are doing." Diawara calls out in the strident tones of one used to being obeyed. "Return all items to the shelves."

A flustered-looking auditor opens his mouth, as though he's actually going to question this. Diawara flashes brilliant white teeth at him. "Mister Faulkes and I are going into business together. Isn't that so, Jerome?"

I look down. From now on, I'm a puppet, my business nothing more than a honeypot to lure high-ranking deviants into giving themselves away.

Sergeant Shamon motions towards the back room behind the counter. I receive another jab from a baton and stumble forward.

The back room is spartan. Empty crates are piled haphazardly against one wall. I lead the party to the small wooden cabinet at the rear of the room.

Diawara frowns. "Is this it? How terribly disappointing, Jerome. I always imagined an arch-deviant such as yourself would have a secret room behind a hidden panel for all your most heretical artefacts."

I want to snort. The so-called purity Diawara and her ilk treasure creates stunted imaginations. Secret panels and similar contrivances are clear signals the owner has something to hide. For this precise reason, my strong box is housed within a dilapidated, mid-twentieth-century drinks cabinet in an empty room, placed in full view of the shop.

When you allow people to see your hiding place, they assume they know where your secrets are kept.

Shamon swears under his breath. "That can't be it. This is bullshit, Jerome." He reaches for one of the cabinet handles. Diawara bats his hand away. "Idiot. It's a quantum-locked vault. If you open this door, it won't be there."

Shamon stares at her. It barely qualifies as a micro-expression, but for one split second, he meets Diawara's golden eyes with an anger approaching defiance. Their shared look is over almost before it has begun. Shamon casts his eyes downwards—the properly subservient attitude of a local militiaman towards a quaestor—but not before something passes between them.

I see a familiar fury in Shamon's glare, an anger born of humiliation, subjugation—

Oh.

The realisation is as wonderful as it is cathartic. I bite down on my tongue to withhold a smile. The iron tang of blood fills my mouth.

Diawara leans forward. "Open it." She motions to one of her companions. "Free his hands."

There's a tug at the plastic binding my wrists as a blade is placed between them. A moment later, the awful constriction of the plastic cuffs is gone. I kneel before the cabinet, rubbing life into my hands.

Quaestor Diawara has been clever. She allowed me to become overconfident, then used the threat to Prudence to panic me, to unpick my defences. In despair, I never once questioned Diawara's suggestion that they had her in custody.

Prudence is not held in a quaestor's cell. The body count required to accomplish her capture alone would have made her otherness plain for all to see. Clever Laurenz Diawara would already have made all the necessary connections in that case. There would be no need for this charade.

If it hadn't been for that single, unspoken moment between Shamon and Diawara, I would have opened the vault before I realised my error.

Diawara saw that a threat to Prudence would unravel my reason when even I did not. I suppose I should thank her for this self-knowledge.

To be loved unconditionally is an extraordinary thing. I wonder that I placed so little value on it before. I'm grateful for the revelation that I too, am capable of such love.

Prudence, if you are safely up there in the darkness, remain still and quiet. Continue to resist that biological urge to keep me close, to protect me. That you've done this till now, seen better than I could the narrow path we must navigate brings a choke to my throat. What happens next is done entirely for you.

Diawara crouches next to me, fixated on the cabinet door that conceals my forbidden vault. I'm supposed to unlock it, reveal the awful alien thing inside, and damn myself.

I place my hand on the wooden door, feeling it grow hot under my touch as a thin scraping of living genetic material is extracted.

"Open it, Faulkes," Diawara hisses in my ear.

The Quaestor came after me to get to someone else, just as she suborned Shamon to get to me. This is how she works, one link in the chain at a time, subverting self-interest to her purpose.

What must Diawara have done to procure that terrible thing Shamon brought me? The bait in her trap is a prohibited object of the highest order. Such things are kept sequestered in secret archives. Even a quaestor would have to call in substantial favours to have it released to their care. Woe betide whoever lost such an object in the field.

I tap the code into the panel on the otherwise smooth metal surface. Beside me, Diawara's breath is shallow and rapid.

The existence of this safe is a sin I will admit to only because it diverts attention from far, far worse crimes. If you own a safe, no one questions where you keep your secrets.

I open the safe door.

Diawara is motionless for several seconds. She rips the sparse contents—a few mouldering copies of the King James Bible and the Qur'an—from the safe and stares at the now-empty interior. "Where is it?" Her voice rises. "Where is the artefact, Faulkes?"

I have nothing to say.

A quantum vault doesn't have to resemble a safe. It's as unnatural a form for an alien technology as anything in the human imagination. A vault could just as easily be an amoeba, a fungi, a cathedral, a gas giant, a supernova—or a girl.

"What have you done with it?" Diawara grabs the lapels of my jacket. "Speak, vermin, or I'll destroy you and that bitch of yours."

I wag a finger slowly and measure the dissolution of self-righteous anger in her twitching expression. The first signs of panic are written momentarily on her features—before the mask of total self-assurance descends once more.

She gave me possession of that terrible little box and now, there is no promise—no sentence, torture, or bribe—which would induce me to surrender the hold I possess over her. Were they ever to learn what she had done, her fellow quaestors would consider Diawara compromised—corrupted, deviant. We would burn together.

Are you still watching and listening, dear Prudence? I have cleaved Laurenz Diawara to me and made our fates indivisible. Understand I have done this because it's the path that ensures your survival.

"Everyone but Faulkes leave this room now." Diawara's voice is calm. She doesn't take her eyes off me as her retinue scurry to obey her. The speed of her adjustment to this new reality is rather admirable. It suggests a greater intellectual flexibility than I'd credited her with.

She cocks her head slightly. "Well, Faulkes, what happens now?"

I smile. "Care to make a deal with the Devil, Quaestor Diawara?"

In the lightless confines of this place, tails coil around one another and become inextricably knotted. We are all corrupt, yet, here in the darkness between the stars, we persist.

Rob Gillham is a British author of dark speculative fiction. He does all his writing in the margins of the day. Rob's work has appeared in Clarkesworld, Escape Pod, Cosmic Horror Monthly, and Creepy Podcast amongst others. Links to all his work and social media can be found at robgillham.com.

Beyond Hearing

Hugh McCormack

My morning began as many had that December. I was hurrying with the other commuters towards Camden Town Station, violin case bouncing on its shoulder strap, phone at my ear. As ever, Dan answered on the second ring.

"Forgot something? Or is it you just can't live without me?"

"Both, of course." He always made me laugh. "I forgot to put lunch in my calendar—and you know how sieve-like my memory is."

Up ahead people were funnelling under the London Underground sign, up the four steps into the concourse.

"Two pm. Don't be late."

"I'll try. But as we're rehearsing for the Christmas concert, you never know what's going to hap—"

I bounced off a man. Just before the steps. A big lump, heavy black coat, face behind a navy balaclava. Something in his canvas shoulder bag smacked hard against my elbow.

"My time now, bitch!"

His snarl quashed my apology. He didn't break stride, didn't glance back, didn't see as I ricocheted into the glossy terracotta-tiled jamb, smudged by street grime, and fell to the frosty pavement, my violin case landing beside me with a hollow clomp.

"Essie?"

Commuters flowed past me up the steps, one or two peering down, as if I was a weirdly misshapen rock in their streambed.

"Essie?"

"I'm here."

"You alright?"

"Yes, it was just one of those people you don't want to meet."

"But you're alright? You don't sound—"

And then it started, and once again my phone seemed to jump from my grasp.

That morning, Essie was late. As usual. She was up early enough, but spent a while carefully wiping her violin before placing it in its case. Then she was rushing back and forth from bedroom to bathroom, whispering to herself as she dropped clothes from drawers, before rushing out of the front door without closing it, coming back a few seconds later, calling "Bye, Dan!" and shutting the door, ever so gently, as she always did.

It was a full ten minutes later when she phoned, and I was already at my desk, preparing for my Zoom meeting with Tom. All she'd forgotten was our lunch date.

Then the world went off-piste.

On the phone, I couldn't tell what was happening, and after the hammering burst of gunfire, I lost the connection. My redials only reached the answerphone.

By the time I approached the tube station, breathing hard, a column of police cars and ambulances lined Kentish Town Road and sirens were screaming into the bitter air. Some people were walking away, but others were standing around the shop windows or by the bank on the corner, looking on, as if waiting for something else to happen. There was no sign of Essie.

Black-and-yellow crime-scene tape barred the station entrance the top of the steps. Inside, a policeman was standing by the ticket barriers. I started shouting at him, but he was on the phone, a hand over his other ear, and above the sirens didn't seem to hear. Or didn't want to know.

Still yelling, I ducked under the tape, advanced on him. But as I came up, a glove landed on my shoulder, and a policewoman was instructing me to get back.

It was another half hour before I discovered anything about Essie.

I was struggling to keep down the eruptions of memories and feelings. I wanted to call Dan, but still didn't have my phone. Although they'd found it at the tube station, they'd kept it for analysis. I knew there were greater things going on here.

I was alone in the waiting room, seated on a plush sofa, elbows on knees, hands clasped together, knuckles white. It was in a restricted section of the hospital, nothing like the rest: small, solid, pale and impersonal. A radio performance of Beethoven's Sixth was being muffle-mangled by cheap speakers, but even worse was the scent of stale lavender that seemed to blanket everything, like a layer of thick purple dust that you couldn't wipe away.

Whenever my mind began to wander, I tried to focus my gaze on something. I stared at my coffee, black and cold in its doubled-up white plastic cups. Into the dark oak grain of the coffee table. Up at the industrial blinds that cut the lurking dark clouds with clean cold lines. Across to the yellow splurgings of a van Gogh sunflowers print pressed inside gleaming glass.

As my eyes wouldn't rest, I closed them and tried to extract Beethoven's genius from the hiss and rasp of the sound system. The woodwind cadenza of the second movement frisked and flourished as it always did, like the carefree birdsong it represented, and for a while I was able to flow with it.

Then it came.

Without warning, a mad banging inside my head, a pneumatic drill. I clamped my hands over my ears, started screaming, but couldn't stop it.

Fragments of memory burst in like shards of glass, slashing, scouring, lacerat—

A hand on my shoulder curbed my screams. An unfamiliar face, concerned, kind eyes looking down, somehow overpowered the banging within me.

"Essie, are you okay?"

I wanted to reassure her, but felt unable speak. So I clasped the hand on my shoulder, squeezed hard, tried to smile.

"I'm Doctor Leah Chamberlain. I'm sorry, you shouldn't have been left alone." She sat down beside me. "You were getting flashbacks?"

I nodded.

"Ultra-realistic? Exaggerated details?"

I nodded again, wiped away a tear. I felt like a lost child.

"The drug does that for some people." She took my hand in both of hers. "But it's only temporary, and will fade quickly once the recording process is over."

"Then… can we start straight away?"

She smiled. "The sooner the better. Are you ready?"

She had such kind eyes.

Eleven-forty-one.

I'd been in the waiting room only five minutes. Unable to sit. I paced from sofa to window. And back again.

Kept looking at my phone.

Eleven-forty-two.

Past the water dispenser, past the weird flower painting.

On my phone, news of the attack streamed in. *Six confirmed dead… dozens injured…*

Essie wasn't one of them, they'd told me. She was unhurt, just helping the investigation in some way. I didn't know why they'd taken her to a hospital.

Eleven-forty-two, still.

Beyond the blinds, the sky was dark, not a patch of blue.

Lone gunman… manhunt underway… appeal for witnesses…

Despite a cup of machine coffee on the table, the room seemed rarely used. The magazine rack was empty except for a copy of the Economist. I recognised its cover and remembered reading it, but that had been months ago.

Eleven-forty-three.

My knee bashed the water dispenser. I swore at it.

Station closed… area sealed off…

Classical music was playing, Mozart or something. The kind of thing that sends me to sleep in no time but which at home Essie listens to for hours on her headphones, lying on the sofa, all the cushions stacked up around her, eyes closed, totally at peace.

Eleven-forty—

The door swung open, and in strode a middle-aged woman in a white coat.

"I'm sorry to keep you waiting. Dan, isn't it?" She offered me her hand, smiling. "I'm Doctor Leah Chamberlain. I'm overseeing the process."

"Essie's here?"

"I've just been with her." Another smile.

"So why is she here, in a hospital? I was told she wasn't hurt."

"That's right. But here's not the place to talk. Let's go to my office."

From the waiting room, she led me up a flight of stairs.

"Can't I see her first?"

"Not yet, I'm afraid."

"But it's been a couple of hours. And her phone's switched off."

"Let's get to my office first, but I can assure you, there's nothing to worry about."

She smiled as she held a door open for me, and we entered a corridor of office doors, each with a plaque on the wall beside it. We passed a uniformed policewoman carrying a thin red file who smiled a good morning to the doctor.

"Essie's a very brave young woman, you know." Yet another smile as she entered the door at the end of the corridor.

I stopped dead when I read the plaque: *Leah Chamberlain, Psychiatrist.*

It felt like I was in a void. I could feel the padded plastic of the couch under my fingers, and the weight of my body pushing down against it, the ache in my left shoulder from the injections, and the press of one or two of the sensors they had attached all over my body. But that was all. My headset controlled what I saw, heard and smelled, and for now it was inactive.

"Essie, can you hear me?"

Leah's voice made me jump.

"Yes, yes. I can."

"We're all set here. Are you ready?"

It was all I could do to stop myself shaking.

"Essie?"

"I… yes, I think so."

"So remember, the recording process will take only ten to twelve minutes, but will probably feel much longer. Then there'll be a recovery period. We'll be monitoring how your body responds, and will terminate the process if anything serious happens. You understand?"

"I think so."

"And when your recovery period is over, you'll be able to see Dan. He's arrived at the hospital, and is making his way to the suite."

Relief rushed through me, and I was about to ask her to give him a message when she spoke again.

"Okay, we're starting. I'll see you in ten minutes."

There was a click and then nothing. Time seemed to drift. Cold crept over my skin, dank air came into my nostrils. Then came a hum, quiet at first, then growing louder. It took on distinct forms. The dirty notes of noise. Traffic noise. Cars, a moped… a bus. And footfalls, many, a pattering of different footwear, like a rhythm section.

Then a man's voice. Dan's voice! His phone voice. In my right ear only, growing steadily louder. But he wasn't articulating any words. It was certainly his voice, his timbre and rhythm, his pitch spectrum, yet slurred and incoherent.

Then I heard words, fuzzy at first, but growing gradually clearer: "For… got… for… got… forgot… forgot… forgot some… something? Forgot… some… thing… some… thing?"

I was smiling. At his voice, at the way he elucidated every word, every syllable, as though he cared for the form of his phonemes.

"Or… or is it… or is… it… it you… you just… just… can't… just can't… can't… live… live… with… without… without me?"

As though he cared about what I heard, recognised my sensitivity to sounds, realised how much his voice meant to me.

"Two… two… two p… m… pm…. Don't be… be… be… don't be… be late… late…"

His voice was my favourite musical instrument. Harmonised my day.

But then it was gone. Suddenly and completely. Only the street sounds remained.

I knew what was coming next. My fingers started clawing at the couch's plastic. Then I was shuddering uncontrollably. As my back arched, one of my nails cut into the plastic, made a hole that I clawed open.

And yet, when it came, the voice was not as bad as I'd feared. Maybe it was because I couldn't see the man, hadn't been whacked by the gun in his bag, hadn't been thrown to the ground.

"My… my… time… my time… now… now… my time now… bitch!… bitch!… bitch!… bitch!"

"When can I see her?" I asked as I sat down.

"Let me check." Across the desk, the doctor peered into one of her screens, shifted her mouse.

It was a tidy desk, large enough for everything to be spaced out. A keyboard, mouse and two screens were on one side, a coffee mug, pad and pen in front of her. There were also two photos; one a face shot of a balding middle-aged man, the other a boy and girl in a dodgem car at a funfair in a glossy blue frame.

"Essie's doing well." The doctor smiled. "She'll be ready in twenty minutes or so."

"But what exactly is she doing?"

"You've not been told?"

"Only that she's helping the police."

"That's all?" She raised her eyebrows. "Well, she's helping to identify the gunman, using a new technique. If everything goes well, she'll be able to return home in a couple of hours."

"What do you mean, 'new technique'?"

"I'm sure you understand, that after any terrorist incident, it's vital to identify the perpetrators as soon as possible. CCTV images can't do this if they're masked, so we've developed a way to identify them from their voice."

"Voice? Can you really do that now?"

"Our forensic scientists have devised a technique to preserve and extract a memory of a voice. They've developed a new drug that creates what we call a 'prolonged eidetic memory', or PEM, an accurate memory of the voice. Then, by using brain-imaging technology, we can extract the PEM from the listener's head. This PEM extraction will be a one-hundred percent accurate recording of the voice. Since a human voice is unique, like a vocal fingerprint, it can be used to identify us. So if we upload the PEM extraction into the country's security systems, we'll have a network of ears to listen out for the perpetrator."

"So what's this to do with Es…" And then I realised. "But you can't give her a drug like that!"

"She agreed to be given it by our officers at the scene. Although it's brand new, it's been comprehensively tested."

"No, you don't understand. She's not the sort of person who can cope with this."

"She's responded perfect—"

"And there was no need to give her a drug. She's a professional musician with perfect relative pitch."

"Yes, she told me. But this goes beyond hearing. It's more about memory. Most people think their memories are a hundred-percent accurate, but they rarely are. That's because we need to integrate our new memories with our older memories, to help us grasp their full significance and understand the big picture. The downside is that the integration distorts the new memory to some extent."

I didn't really follow this, but the implication was clear to me: "So the drug messes with her memory, not her hearing?"

"No, Dan. It's not like that at all. It has a very specific and focused effect; it just enables the PEM to form."

"Then why would Essie need a psychiatrist? She's not mad!"

"I trained as a psychiatrist, but my specialty is post-traumatic stress disorder, such as the effects of witnessing a terrorist attack."

"But Essie… She's not a… good fit for this."

"I think you're underestimating her. In any case, we've developed strict protocols for the drug's safe use and we're monitoring her very—"

"No, it's you who doesn't understand. She's just... she's not cut out to be involved in this sort of thing. If you knew her, you'd know I'm right."

I jumped up from the sofa when Dan rushed into the recovery lounge. As I held him, Angie, the policewoman, slipped out of the room. I just wanted to listen to his breath, ragged though it was, to cling onto the bulk of his body, tense though it was, to feel the soft curls on my cheek, to allow the smells of his aftershave and shampoo to linger in my nose.

"I'm okay," I said into his ear. "Really okay. Leah says they just need to do one last test. If it's good, I can go home tonight, and I'll be able to make the last two rehearsals. Wouldn't that be great?"

"Yeah, she told me. That's good news."

But he was distracted. So distracted I realised I shouldn't tell him about the buzzing noise. It would only worry him more, and, in any case, I hadn't heard it for many minutes.

When I finally let him pull away, he handed me a large white plastic bag. At that moment, I couldn't think what it might be, but as soon as I pulled out a huge box of chocolates, I realised it couldn't have been anything else.

"Rations for a year?" I asked, sitting back down on the sofa.

"The smallest box in the shop."

I almost laughed.

"Did you bring my headphones?"

"I... I'll bring them later."

"It's really imp..."

I gulped, felt the tears coming. Why did he never seem to remember what was important to me? Then his arms were around me again, and my hands clung at folds of his shirt.

"I'm really glad I did it," I whispered.

When he didn't reply, I thought maybe he hadn't heard. Then I realised: he disapproved.

"We're all just so fragile, so defenceless." My voice felt weak, unconvincing, but I had to make him understand. "All these attacks. Will they ever stop? You remember that docudrama we saw, a couple of weeks back, with that lorry driving through the school playground? The children unable to get out of the way. When they blanked out the screen but we still heard the children? Even now I can hear their screams."

"But they must have pressured you to help them."

"Not at all. Don't you see? I have to do my bit. I just can't let everyone down!"

He pulled away, looked towards the window.

Tentatively, I touched his arm. "Had you been there, maybe you'd understand. I just want to make a difference. I know I'm usually too... indecisive to do something like this. But someone has to stop them. And Leah said I was amazing. The recording they got was better than anything they got when they were testing the drug."

He turned back, but his eyes were seething.

"You have to put yourself first! I've told you often enough. You don't have to suffer for others."

"But I haven't suffered, not really. I had a long chat with Leah. She's really nice and really reassured me, that I'll soon be back to normal."

He contracted his eyebrows. "However nice she seems, you can't trust her. You know that, don't you?"

That was when the buzzing noise returned. The drone of that man's voice, distorted echoes of his words. Reverberating through my head. Flushing me with his hatred. Flooding me with fear. Reminding me of my helplessness. And of what would come next.

I reached out to Dan, held him as tightly as I could.

"Tell me about your day." My voice quivered, struggled to rise above the buzzing. "What did Tom say... about your plan for the new year?"

"We've... I pulled out of our meeting."

"Tell me about the plan."

"I've already told you every—"

"Tell me again."

As before, he lost me with the financial particulars, all those terms I didn't understand. But that didn't really matter. I only wanted to hear his voice, the way it fashioned his words in a soothing soundscape, the way it fuzzed and foamed like wavelets washing a beach. I should really tell him sometime, how much his voice calms me, how it softens all the harsh edges of my life. Yet that afternoon his enthusiasm for his plan was muted, and the pacifying power of his voice failed to nullify the buzzing noise.

So when he paused, I interjected:

"Dan, you will help me through this, won't you?"

Striding ahead of the receptionist, I barged through the door. As the doctor looked up, started to smile, I slammed my file down on her desk. I'd long ago discovered the authority of heavy files, even when their paper was blank.

"Essie's now been here a day and a half! Yesterday, you said it'd be two hours."

The doctor seemed unmoved. Her smile had gone, and a hand signal dismissed the receptionist lingering in the doorway, but otherwise she just held my gaze, as though waiting for my next move.

"You have to let her out!"

"You're right, Dan, of—"

"When? When will you let her out?"

"Please sit down and we'll talk about it."

She motioned to the chair. I hesitated, then complied. For now, I had to play by her rules.

"I've good news." She smiled. "The scans and psychometric tests we've done today show that the flashbacks have stopped and the PEM is breaking down."

"So she can go home now?"

"We have to proceed carefully. This is a new drug and—"

"But she'll be much happier at home, more relaxed. She'll have her things, all her music."

She took a deep breath. "Please, Dan, let me explain. It's a new drug, in what we call third-phase testing, and it's always possible to see another unexpected reaction. We've already had one with Essie."

I hated her monotonous, self-assured tone. "You mean, the drug wasn't tested properly?"

"No, Dan, the testing was comprehensive. It's just that people are complex and respond in different ways. With Essie, memories of sounds are more central in her mind, making more connections and enduring longer. This is probably because she has a particularly refined sensitivity to sounds, and—"

"I told you: she has perfect relative pitch."

"Yes, I realise there's—"

"You should've listened!" I hated the way she ignored the obvious. "Adjusted your treatment."

"All our interventions are personalised, and Essie's very open with me, tells me everything I need to know."

"I doubt that."

For a moment, we glared at each other. She might be a psychiatrist, but, like everyone else, could still be taken in. Maybe she was beginning to see that.

"But now—"

"That's why she should be at home. I know her. All her quirks. Her needs. All the things you have to ask her about, and hope she tells you."

The doctor took another deep breath. "It'll help her to be at home, especially over Christmas. I agree with that. But in this phase of her recovery, it's really important that we all work together to make it as smooth and quick for her as possible. So for several days you'll need to be there, in case she—"

"I'm not going anywhere."

"You'll also need to ensure she has no reminders of the attack. So don't start a conversation about it, or watch the news, or go to crowded places, or anything else that—"

"I wasn't born yesterday!"

"It's very important, because there's a high risk of a panic reaction."

"I do know how to look after her, you know."

"You'll also have to monitor her symptoms. With the PEM breaking down, the buzzing will also recede, but it's imp—"

"What buzzing?"

She raised her eyebrows. "She's not told you?"

I glared at her, but said nothing. Maybe this would give me the leverage I wanted.

"She's been experiencing an intermittent buzzing in her ears, like echoes or fragments of the PEM. This also happened to some testees as the PEM broke down, but for all of them it disappeared after—"

I jumped to my feet.

"The drug's messed up her head!"

I picked up my file…

"Dan, please—"

…and crashed it down on the desk.

"And yet you do nothing!"

I jabbed my finger right at her, and she shrank back into her chair

"You don't even care about her, do you!"

The desk shuddered as I leant right across it, causing the photos in their pretty frames to fall over.

"You only care that she catches your terrorist for you!"

"He's been caught!" Her voice was shrill, even gleeful.

"What?"

"At Birmingham Airport, identified from his voice. It was all down to the PEM extraction." She beamed at me. The cat who had stolen the cream.

"I don't care." And I really didn't.

"Maybe not, but Essie was overjoyed to hear. She told me catching him vindicated her decision to help us."

I laughed as I pulled back from the desk, stood up straight. "She only said that because she knew you'd want to hear it. And because she wants you to let her out. And with him caught, you've no reason to keep her here any longer, have you?"

Klaus wasn't singing. There was no spontaneity, no flow. The entrances to the notes grated, as if my bow was a blunt knife, carving them off him. He had his moods, but this one was new.

And Mendelssohn didn't deserve it.

The recovery lounge wasn't the best place for Klaus, of course. It was too small, with a hard laminate floor and lots of furniture. Sounds reverberated and echoed. But at home the acoustics were just as bad and Klaus was never like this.

I switched to Brahms.

After a minute or so of the concerto's first movement, I stopped. It wasn't merely that Klaus wasn't singing; he was different somehow. His tone had changed, as if he'd acquired an accent, or was mimicking someone else's voice.

I put him down on the coffee table, laid the bow beside him, slumped down on the brown-leather sofa. Taking a deep breath, I tried to relax, embrace the silence.

Maybe he was sick; it was a hospital, after all. Or maybe he was sulking and just needed more love.

I was still cleaning him when Leah entered the lounge. With her warm smile and kind eyes everything seemed suddenly brighter.

"How's it going?"

I shrugged. "My violin needs even more TLC than usual. It helps if I clean it."

She sat down beside me. "How's the hearing?"

"Fine." I put on my best smile.

"The buzzing?"

"Leaving me alone, still." I was pushing the cloth into Klaus' right f-hole, and even though I could have done this blindfold, I kept my eyes fixed on the task. Dan had often told me I wasn't a good liar, but if I avoided eye contact maybe I'd fool her.

"Nothing this morning?"

I shook my head, peering into Klaus's yellow-brown sheen as I switched to his left f-hole.

For a moment, Leah didn't say anything, and when I looked up, her face was giving nothing away.

Then she smiled. "Well, that's the confirmation I needed. The tests all show you're recovering, and I'm sure it will only accelerate when you're back home."

"Home? When?"

"As soon as I've done your care plan."

I glanced at Klaus, to gauge his reaction. I knew I should be happy.

"Is something wrong?" She touched my arm.

"It's just nerves." I dared to look up into the kindness of her eyes.

"Are you worried about how it will be at home?" Seriousness edged her concern. "At home with Dan?"

"With Dan? No, of course not. I've a concert on Boxing Day. It's being recorded for radio, and so many friends and family are going to be there. I'm so relieved I won't let them down."

I heard the violin as I hurried towards the recovery lounge. It was the piece called Spring that Essie often played when she was happy.

Just as I reached the open door, she stopped playing. She was standing motionless near a sofa, hair pulled up in a high ponytail, staring down at her violin.

"Essie!"

Her kiss was short, her embrace not much longer.

"What's wrong?"

"Too many cobwebs."

I could never tell how well she played.

"Maybe it's just a little early for Spring?"

"Maybe that's it." But she didn't even smile. "I'll be better tomorrow, when I'm out of here, when I'm in the hall with the others."

I sat down on a sofa. "Why don't you play something else?"

She opened her mouth for a moment, as if about to object, then smiled faintly. When she raised her violin to her shoulder, she started a slower, sadder piece.

Although classical music bored me, I always liked watching her play. The way she kept her eyes closed, swinging her violin in exaggerated sideways movements, bending backwards and forwards from the waist, only occasionally moving her feet. It was the way she always played, and reassured me that she was returning to normal.

As the music meandered on, I checked my texts. Tom had confirmed our rearranged Zoom meeting. Mel was asking where to meet for Essie's concert. Ben had sent pictures of breakfasting at his Paris hotel. The solicitor had confirmed our—

Essie was motionless, like a statue. She still held her violin horizontally, bow hovering above it, eyes and mouth closed.

It was only when she opened her eyes that I saw the tears.

I followed Dan out of the hospital's main door into the cold fresh air, my violin case bouncing on its shoulder strap. I was still hopeful.

I stopped, listened. And my hopes wilted.

The wheeze of the distant traffic was too harsh, echoed unnaturally in my head. Then, when two nurses passed me, chatting away, their voices seemed shrill, scraped at my ears.

Dan was already striding across the hospital carpark, not even glancing back for me. I knew he was stressed by what had happened, but it was a bad time for another one of his moods. He was already sitting in the driver's seat when I reached the car, staring forward into the distance, and didn't seem to notice when I slipped in.

The car was no warmer than outside. When I pulled my door, it clunked shut, as if I'd pulled it harder than normal. When my seatbelt clacked harshly, I examined the clasp, but it looked the same as always.

"At least I can make the final rehearsal. I still…" My voice too was affected: tinny, vacuous, lost.

Maybe it was down to the winter cold. Maybe it would ease over time. Maybe in the hall, with its acoustics, when we all started playing.

The car engine coughed into a moan, dropped down to a tutting muttering, as if it shared Dan's mood.

"I still have a couple of hours, easily enough time to change and get there."

"If you're up to it." Dan glanced across, forced a smile. "Maybe it's better to relax at home. Or we could go for a walk on the Heath?"

"No, I can't miss it. I can't let them down."

He didn't reply. The engine groaned and growled as we pulled off.

"You'll drive carefully, won't you?"

"Don't I always?"

It was what he always said. Yet his voice, with its soft soundscape, its soothing consonance, had acquired rough edges.

I might have left the hospital, but the malady was still with me, and getting worse; the whole world had gone out of tune.

When I didn't reply, he turned on his music.

It wasn't loud, but rap always felt so intense, and now its relentless staccato juddered into me. I wanted him to turn it off, but knew it calmed him.

Outside, the world drifted by: a parade of Victorian terraced houses, bay windows and patterned brickwork, as sedate and stately as ever. Then the shops with their bold Christmas pitches. And the shoppers crowding the pavement.

Not something I wanted to see.

I closed my eyes.

The rapper's bark swelled up. Nattering, pattering, battering.

I felt the gear shifts as the car accelerated, the sway as it cornered. Dan was driving fast. As usual.

So I turned to the rapper's voice. It surged up, entwined me, dragged me into its dance.

It trampled the tunelessness of the world, quashed its malady.

Soon the rhythms were conducting me. Pulling me, pushing me. This way and that.

Everything else was drowned out.

Not far now. Just a few minutes.

I glanced across at Essie. Her eyes were closed, her face taught, her hands clinging to her seatbelt. It was as if she was too afraid to look at the passing world. The drug was doubtlessly still messing with her head.

My anger surged again. The way they had exploited her desire to help, played down how much she would suffer, tricked her into giving her consent. And the drug hadn't been properly tested. And that doctor, so smug, so blind to what was really going on. Despite all my efforts. She couldn't even tell when Essie was lying. And then, she'd started doubting I could look after Essie!

The sooner we were home, the better. On the GPS, Camden High Street was green, so I went that way. The pavements on both sides were heaving with last-minute Christmas shoppers but the road was traffic free. At least I could still trust the GPS.

I pushed the accelerator. We would soon be back. And then I would have to tell Essie not to go to her rehearsal. I knew it would end in tears, but it had to be done. She had to be protected. I had to get things back to normal.

And then she had to be compensated. The solicitor had said we had a good case. I knew she wouldn't want to, but she was always like that, preferring to suffer in silence whenever someone exploited her.

I turned up the music.

Hugh McCormack is a nonfiction writer/editor branching out into fiction, based in London, UK. His recent publications include stories in Water Dragon Publishing's Dragon Gems anthology (Winter 2024), Twenty-two Twenty-eight and Loft.

The Darkness on Ferrous Street

Quinn J. Graham

The boy was the Devil's kid. That's all anyone cared to know him as anyways. True, maybe his daddy was human when he'd planted that seed, but something dark had shaped that kid, even in the womb.

You hear stories. Stories about how his father died in prison the day he was born. How the nurses wouldn't go near the nursery at night because a baby whispered their names in the dark. Rumours from years ago, but rumours get around.

I didn't know any of that when I moved into Ferrous Street, so I also didn't know that his building was just across from mine. It probably wouldn't've mattered if I'd heard anyway; the rent was cheap, and ghost stories about some weird kid wouldn't have scared me away. I was setting out, looking to start my own life.

Now if I had *met* the kid … I might've changed my mind.

I was on my way to my first day at the mill when I spied him. He was maybe ten or eleven, sitting on the front steps of that tiny, off-yellow apartment building, watching pigeons in the middle of the quiet road. He was tall and lanky, the sort of all-knees-and-elbows kid that looks like a free-fall Jenga tower, wearing nothing but a loose red shirt and shorts. His hair--short, coarse, and frizzy--was white. And his eyes … I only ever got a proper look when he caught me staring.

Do you remember snow days when you were a kid? Everything outside unrecognizable under a thick, muffling blanket of white; the sky that hard sort of grey, like stone? And there was nothing out there, no cars, no people, no birds, no nothing. Just quiet and cold. That deep cold that cuts in right to the bone; makes you think you might freeze just by touching the glass of the window.

I thought about days like that every time I saw his eyes.

But I had to catch the tram, so I left, trying not to shudder as I walked away.

That tram carries a lot of the neighbourhood; most of us don't have cars, and it's the easiest way over the river cutting through the city. It's not a long ride, but there's always talk about so-and-so's kid, or what-his-face's new job colouring the clatter of the wheels. I tended to keep to myself--no need to go mucking in other people's business--but even my ears pricked when eventually talk turned to the Ferrous Street kid.

"Y'hear about Marty?" someone would say, explaining how Marty, or Darren, or Lucy ran into the 'kid with the eyes.' How he told them to 'watch out,' or that he was 'sorry' for something. Then Marty would get hit by a car, or Darren would run on a bad cop. Lucy gets a call from the hospital, and her mom...

You get the picture.

The word was not to mess with him. Don't let your children near him. If he was coming your way, take a side street. I couldn't blame them; every day, he was always on those steps, occupying a street otherwise as empty as an open grave. I'd look anywhere else when I went on my way, but he never seemed to leave me. At work, I could feel his stare like a pair of icicles stuck in my back, and when he watched me come home, a freezing gaze followed me, even after I was alone in my apartment, and I had dreams of blizzards with sterile, uncaring eyes.

There's a bar at the end of Ferrous Street, just around the corner on Kerlic Avenue. Follow the stone steps down to the steel door, and you'll be at the Floating Crone. It's a tight little space, but it serves well enough as a watering hole. The first time I went was after work one day. I knew the kid would be outside like always, and the chills I got when he looked at me were becoming too hard to bear, but I figured even devil-children had curfews. I decided to wait him out with a detour on my route home.

I was surprised to find most of the fellas from the tram coming with me. It was habit for them, the local hang-out to unwind after long hours, and the conversations from the ride home continued well into their second, third, and fourth drinks.

They all hated him, and booze only fueled the fire. One of them saw a boy, about the kid's own age, seizure at a word from the kid's mouth. Another swore he saw lights, will-o-wisps, flash between the boy's palms when he thought no one was looking. A grey-bearded man, weary face buried in the palm of one hand with a bottle snug in the other, moaned that he didn't know what to do about his daughter, who kept asking questions about the boy no matter how many times he told her to drop it.

It wasn't any different to what I heard on the tram--just guys swapping gab 'cause they had nothing better to do. But now I wasn't eavesdropping on conversations from two or three seats away; I was in the circle, stories bouncing between all of us like echoes in a tunnel. It didn't help me forget about the kid, but like a hand squeezing my shoulder, it told me I wasn't alone.

When I left the Crone hours later, the kid was nowhere to be seen, and I entered my quiet apartment untroubled, sleep coming easily for the first time in days.

That became the new routine. Wake up, go to work, the Crone, and home. It brought me peace some, helped me deal with what lived in the building across the way, but it couldn't erase it completely. Like I said earlier, the tram goes over the river, and a little later on the ride home, I glanced out the window.

And there he was.

There's a small, gravel shore at the river's edge, a worn concrete staircase that juts out from the bulkhead bridging it and the streets above, and that's where I saw the kid. And he was doing something.

The river wall, like a lot of the neighbourhood, is covered in graffiti, and the kid was adding his own. I only got the smallest glance, but it wasn't a tag; it was a girl.

She's painted in thick lines of black on a white mist of spray paint. Her long hair is trapped in the same frozen breeze as her sundress, which ends just above her ankles and bare feet. She looked older than him, obvious from her height, but not by much. Her hands were held behind her back, and even from above, through the dust and dirt-speckled glass of the tram window, I could see that she was smiling.

Then we passed overhead, and the duo disappeared.

I started seeing him on that little gravel beach everyday after that. He would sit, draw on the ground, splash ankle-deep in water that I'm sure was freezing no matter the weather. But sometimes he'd stare at the girl. Sometimes I thought I could see his mouth moving, but just as we got close enough to be sure, they're swallowed by the street at the end of the bridge. I'm plopped back into the tram, surrounded by sweaty, tired, and cranky men who after weeks I recognized only by face--brothers and strangers.

In all the story-swapping at the Crone, I never shared what I saw of the kid on the river. It was kid stuff. The kid didn't do kid stuff. We all knew that.

But now we were tired of stories, and as a tall fella wrapped up his account of the kid to an applause of grunts, another man who kept his head down most nights stepped to the mound with a curve ball.

"We oughta do something about him."

There was an uncomfortable chuckle from a few of them, but when the speaker didn't join in, silence draped over us like a sheet. No one looked at anything but their drinks, faces blank. They were all thinking the same thing, and I know because I thought it too; long before it had ever been spoke, the idea had a presence among us. The rest of us were just too scared to acknowledge it. But now the monster had been dragged out from under the bed, and we could poke and prod at it all we liked.

It spurred conversation. The loudest would talk about the things they'd do to him--baseball bats and fists--and the quiet ones talked on how they wouldn't be caught. The man with the curious daughter, who still asked about the boy constantly, had a plan so involved that it spoiled my appetite. Even I spun a yarn about feeling the kid's throat under my fingers, and after, when I was in my apartment and the warmth of company had given way to isolation's silence, the words would echo in my head, sounding as if they'd come from a stranger.

Still, it was mostly just show. Devil-child or not, a kid's disappearance would bring flashing lights and badges, and that could be an even bigger boogeyman than the one we knew to live nearby. But it was fun for them to imagine a dream where they were the ones to make the world normal again.

There was a tipping point. A storm was due to come in one evening--big one too. None of us met up at the Crone that night.

That curious daughter of the grey-bearded fella, she didn't know about it until the clouds grew dark and wind rattled the glass in the windows. And her first thoughts turned to the boy, who, with her interest in him, she knew spent time at the river. By the time she'd put on her coat and her boots and had left for the boy's gravel shore, the rain was like iron pellets, and buildings moaned as gusts tore their way through the streets.

She was found floating a few miles downstream the next day.

Her father got the news while we were all together, through the phone, the poor bastard. His wail flowed up from the stomach, pouring into the air like the man's own guts as the tears fell. The rest of us only watched as he sobbed, eyes screwed, body thrown against the bar like a great heaving rag doll, and in the quiet that underscored the howling, a dark cloud gathered between us. When our eyes weren't fixed on the crying man or the floor, they met with each other.

We had all heard about the interest the girl took in the boy; we all knew what must've happened.

No one said anything, but when the father's cries slowed enough, he led the charge. The sun had just set, and we marched towards the river.

I swear he was waiting for us. We came to the head of the concrete staircase and found him down there, standing with his feet in the freezing waters, looking out to the other shore. A dozen or more pairs of work boots thudded down the steps, and only when the mob was right behind him did he turn around.

There was snow in his stare, an ice-cold certainty. I don't know how, but he knew what was about to happen. He'd known for a while.

Shivers played on my spine.

There was only a second's hesitation before the first fella grabbed him and pushed him down. It might've been the father. It could've been somebody else; I don't remember, and I don't remember who the other two were who joined in either. What I remember is being frozen. While they held him under, I was sure those snow-day eyes were staring up at me through the ripples, and I couldn't move a muscle.

When they let him go, the water began to carry him away. There was quiet as we watched him float on, an uncertainty, as if there should have been something more. But as the night deepened, and the boy's body disappeared down the river, uncertainty turned to uneasiness, and none of us could stand to be there any longer. As the rest of the group turned to go, I caught a glimpse of the grey-bearded father's face. He watched the spot where the boy vanished longer than any of us, and as he came to join the group again, fresh tear trails shone on his face.

He passed me on the way to the stairs, and when I followed I saw the boy's graffiti, the girl he painted on the wall. None of the others had noticed, but after seeing her from the tram time and time again I was entranced by my first close-up view. Her arms were at her sides as her hair and dress billowed in that invisible breeze, and she smiled just like always. But there was something different this time, something I would have never noticed if I hadn't seen her before; I couldn't ever remember her smile looking that strained.

One of the others had to pull me away before I could move again, and we left, separating at the top of the stairs, unsure of what would come in the morning.

The answer, as it turned out, was nothing. There were no reports about another body in the river; no police turned up at my door. There weren't even any sirens.

He never appeared at the foot of those steps or on that little gravel beach again. Over the next few days, I walked a quiet sidewalk, into a quiet building, and into my quiet apartment.

I said goodbye to the Crone. With the boy gone, I wasn't afraid of an early trip home anymore, but it also didn't take long to realize that there wasn't anything there but empty silence. I checked in with the guys once, looking for levity, but it was clear something had changed. There was no conversation, or jokes, or laughs. I could barely look at them; every time I tried reminded me of the trickle of the river and the silence of the boy under the water, the sight hanging in front of me like a veil.

I paid for my drinks and left. Haven't been back since.

Then it started happening.

I was leaving for work, but as I stepped out onto the sidewalk I heard whispering. It was a loud whisper, the sort of hissing that comes from something too terrible to say and too tragic to say nothing at all. A crowd had gathered across the street, surrounding the steps of the boy's apartment building.

My heart started beating faster. Sweat was forming on my forehead in the cool of the early morning. Had we been found out? Had the kid come back from the dead? I told myself that couldn't be, but every story I'd heard about him at the bar flashed through my head then, and I found my feet carrying me across the road.

I slid between shoulders, catching bits of gossip.

"...*found him here...*"

"...*drowned, I think...*"

"...*used to live nearby...*"

Every word speared my chest, threatening to pop my heart as it pounded, until I muscled my way to the front of the throng.

There was a body, but it wasn't the boy. At the foot of the stairs, clothes soaked in stinking water, nose and mouth leaking fluid onto the pavement, was the grey-bearded father from our group.

I couldn't feel my heart anymore. I couldn't feel anything. The gawking crowd faded around me, leaving just me and the body, my mind collapsing like a cave-in as I tried to figure out how this could have happened. I looked around, as if the answer could've been lying on the ground.

It wasn't on the ground; it was on the wall. And as soon as I looked up to see it my entire body froze.

Thick black lines painted on a hazy cloud of white, like a solid winter flurry. Feet bare and dress and hair caught in a motionless wind. And that smile, as always.

I broke from the crowd as quickly as I could without attracting attention, down to the tram stop--away from her. I didn't know how the painted girl had done it, but the 'why' was obvious, and I was scared for what might come next.

Days passed, and it got harder to keep myself together. I'd ride to work, only to notice a usual commuter absent--always one of *our* group. The following morning, there would be another crowd at the steps across the street.

I stopped going to work. I holed up inside of my apartment, because maybe the walls would keep me safe at least. But I still had windows. I saw when the police got involved, and the numbers of cruisers on the road outside multiplied from one to two to four, and the way beat cops and detectives alike scratched their heads at how bodies drowned in the river wound up half a mile away, always in the same spot with no one seeing nothing.

I tried the curtains, but that made things worse. Cut off from the world outside, my imagination ran, wondering about what the body count was while I felt the hours and minutes until my eventual turn slip away like sand in an hourglass. How many of the group from the Crone were still around? Did they know what was happening? The more I thought about them, the more I needed to be back in that bar before any of this had happened, when regardless of age we were all old men complaining about how much better the world used to be. Then I would open my eyes, see the empty, cavernous rooms of my home, and realize I was alone, and the feeling of persecution would loom over me like a wave about to crash.

That's when my thoughts turned to the boy, and that final look he'd given us. Given me, maybe. He had known what was about to happen. I was sure.

Was this what he had felt like? Knowing his death was less than ten minutes away?

I thought about him on the steps where the bodies now lay, him and I locking eyes as we stood on opposite sides of the street. And it struck me that for all I had heard of him, I knew nothing. Not a single thing he did, said, or felt was solid in my mind--just shapes I had seen in smoke clouds blown in my face by others. Others who had wanted him dead. Had made me want him dead.

That's when I got up and left.

It should've been raining, but the night sky was just dark, and the police across the street, keeping an eye on the scene, didn't even really watch me go by. I paid them no mind either; I knew where it was I had to go.

She was already there when I started down the concrete steps, as if she'd never been anywhere else.

Nearby, the river flowed, the surface of the water twinkling with the lights of buildings across the way, like a warped reflection of the stars dancing as the water rushed past, and just beneath them, motionless, was a cold darkness. I stepped to the shore, gravel crunching underfoot as I turned my back to her.

Then I closed my eyes.

I might have heard a step behind me. Then nothing. No sound but the constant murmur of the water.

So I did the only thing I could think to do.

"I'm sorry," I said. "I know I wasn't one of them who held him under, but that's an excuse; I didn't do anything, but I should have. Said something, held someone back, something. I'm sorry."

The words welled up in my throat, and so did the shame and self-loathing. The memories of that night and all the nights previous flashed before me, and they now seemed to peel back and reveal something I already knew--sadness and hatred, the pathetic nature of a man who plots with vengeful men to kill a boy he doesn't know.

A question brought itself to my lips.

"What was his name?" I said.

No response.

"Please, I have to know."

The river trickled by. Overhead, a late tram rumbled along the tracks.

The words came out shuddering. "Who did I kill?"

Again, silence. My eyes cracked open. The view in front of me was unchanged. I turned around.

The girl was the same. The wall was not. In the dim glow of the evening, the runoff from the street lamps above, I saw a word written on the concrete surface in black paint that I was sure hadn't been there before:

DESMOND

I had never heard it used, but the name fit. Desmond, like a missing puzzle piece. Desmond, the name of the boy I had murdered.

I looked from his name to her face, the frozen features rendered with the same black paint. My mouth felt dry. "My name is Frank."

The words were quiet, but as the last traces of them disappeared in the chill air, there was a beat. Like the stillness of the night had flickered, and a single heartbeat pulsed through the ground and shook the buildings before it all went quiet again.

She moved.

It was like I forgot where I was, or that I was even there at all. The smile finally fell, the frozen hair and dress too, and I could only watch as she raised two fingers and trailed them through the space next to her, leaving a path of black paint on the wall as they moved, like she was painting on a pane of glass. And when she was finished, two new words rested under Desmond's name.

TANYA.

I read them slowly, and remembered to breathe. "Desmond was your friend?"

She nodded. Her expression, no longer static, was unreadable--equally angry, upset, curious. It took none above the others, a murkiness of emotion.

"Was he a good friend?" I asked.

More writing. BEST FRIEND.

My eyes fell from her. In the gravel I saw nothing. Disappointment shot through me, as if I expected to see answers down there, the pebbles on that shore to rearrange themselves into every thought, or dream, or grief Desmond ever felt--his entire life spelled out in clear terms. In the end, the stones remained still, and his life forever lost to me.

Almost. I raised my head back to Tanya. "Can you tell me about him?"

Desmond's mom had been distant, and he never heard or knew much about his dad after he went away. He didn't have people to talk to about the things he sometimes saw--things that hadn't happened yet--or have anyone who appreciated his attempts to warn them of the tragedies coming their way.

Desmond made Tanya then. Her life had been a surprise to them both, but afterwards he would retreat to the comfort of his only friend when the world was eager to push him away.

Desmond never made graffiti again after Tanya, but he liked to draw pictures for her in the gravel. He liked to hang out on the steps outside his apartment because he didn't like the smell of the cigarette smoke inside.

The walls in Desmond's room were painted a bright baby blue, his favourite food on Earth was chicken strips; and though he didn't usually read, he loved Rapunzel. He'd read it to Tanya a few times, but he never explained why he liked it so much. Often instead of speaking at all, he would stare at the illustrations, running his thumb over the image of the princess being rescued from her tower.

Desmond had seen us coming before we arrived that night, and wanted to spend his last moments with the only person he cared about, and who cared about him. He hadn't burdened her with the knowledge.

The sun rose on Desmond's biography under the bridge, as penned by Tanya in black paint, scoring the wall with dozens and dozens of lashed out sentences, big and bold with tiny details scribbled in the gaps between the letters. It was a mural of words written where they would fit, the order incomprehensible to anyone other than its author, and me, their audience.

I was sitting on the ground now, stones prickling my hands as I leaned back on my arms. Tanya sat in front of me, looking along at the wall-sized epitaph. Beside me was a presence, one that made itself known through an absence that I knew would never leave.

My voice cracked with dryness. "I'm sorry that he's gone."

Tanya nodded without looking my way.

Then she fixed me with a curious gaze for a moment before moving to write again.

I THINK, she began, and then paused. Her fingers trailed to the beginning, as if to cross the words out, but she just stared at them with her mouth in a line for what may have been a minute.

And suddenly she kept writing.

I THINK HE WOULD'VE LIKED YOU, she finished.

Those walks to and from the tram, when Desmond was out on his steps, flew by in an instant, and the cold I always felt from his gaze turned from freezing dread into a longing for warmth. Perhaps as they always had been.

I think I would've liked him too.

I said as much then, as I always do now when talk turns to Desmond. Tanya and I catch up every so often, in new places so she has space to write everything that's happened since our last chat, our conversations scrawled across brick and stone throughout the city.

I see the gang from the Crone in passing, and only in parts. I can still recognize some of them through wrinkles and haggard faces. I think they recognize me back, but whenever our eyes meet, I start to hear the sounds and smell the scents of river water, and we both look away, knowing we experienced the same hallucination.

On the days when Tanya and I meet, and sometimes on the days in between, I dream. I'll be leaving for work as I always do, and he'll be there across the street. I'll sit with him, we talk or we don't talk, but eventually I have to go. When I wake, whatever words passed between us disappear, but the warmth in me remains.

Quinn J. Graham is a writer whose daily life cycles through dogs, video games, reading, and writing in that order. Their fiction has previously appeared in The Dark Sire Literary Journal and On Spec Magazine, and their story 'The Necessity of a Shepherd,' was recently a finalist in the Alberta Magazine Awards. Find them on Bluesky @officialqjg.bsky.social

NewGen

Liam Hogan

Harry Carmichael was going to live forever.

Just as long as his money didn't run out first. At a million dollars for each and every year's treatment, NewGen's immortality didn't come cheap. But that was the half the point, as much as anything else. If you were the sort of person who earned enough to spend seven figures every twelve months on an ethically dubious medical procedure, then obviously you *deserved* to live forever.

Harry Carmichael had been that sort of person for just under two decades. People always need locks and Carmichael locks were, everyone agreed, the best in the industry. He'd moved with the times; a perspective living forever forced upon you. Electronic locks, biometric locks, locks that knew who you were before you even got to the door.

Good old fashioned hardened steel mechanicals were still his bread and butter. It was five-pin tumblers with anti-pick plates that paid for his annual treatment and left just enough to live a relatively comfortable life, after alimony and taxes.

Last year his profits had been so healthy, he'd been tempted to buy NewGen treatment for his newly installed fourth wife, April. But what if that selfless generosity cost him a year of his life, later on? Good times didn't last forever--another lesson the long-lived learned fast. Harry sighed. He should never have mentioned the idea in the first place. April had been all excited, all loving and adorable, until she'd opened the elegant little box he gave her on her birthday. Never had a diamond necklace been met with such abject disappointment.

He'd tried to point out that she was still younger--biologically, as well as chronologically--than he was, but that hadn't gone down well. "I don't *want* to be your age!" she'd raged and, after only a moment's thought, Harry agreed. Nor did he. He hadn't missed a year's treatment in the last nineteen, but he should, he knew, have started much earlier. It would have meant sacrifices; borrowing against an uncertain future, perhaps even one fewer marriage, but it would have been worth it, in the long run. Waiting until he could definitely afford treatment meant he showed his age--his biological age--all forty-two years, the lines and the grey permanently etched.

At least he wasn't getting any older, he consoled himself as he sat in the Head Quarters of NewGen, waiting for his twentieth postponement of fate, for another round of injections to hold back the cruel hands of time for one year longer.

The walls of the reception room displayed glossy adverts never seen in newspapers, on billboards, or on the side of a bus. Adverts individually targeted only when you reached and surpassed a certain income bracket. Before then, Harry had only heard the faintest rumour of NewGen's existence. He gazed up at the posters with an odd sense of nostalgia.

There was the teaser ad; the first to mysteriously appear in the pigeon hole at his private members club. A smiling scientist holding aloft the NewGen logo--a double helix twisted into a sideways eight. There were no contact details, no further clues as to what the product was for. It had been followed, before the eventual hand-written invitation to a personal consultation, by pictures of a young man shaking the hands of a much older colleague, a banner proclaiming: "Happy Retirement".

It had taken Harry a while to work out which of the two men was retiring.

He blushed at his naivety, even while he recognised the obvious falsehood. No-one on NewGen's treatment *ever* retired. Why would you? That would mean you could no longer afford the exclusive and prohibitively expensive procedure. Keep working, keep paying for the treatment, keep hoping you never go bust...

After only a few minutes--time was money, after all--Harry was shown into a discrete office. It wasn't the usual treatment room and Harry's heart thudded in his chest. At a desk, instead of a doctor in a white coat, a gray jacketed woman tapped a slim monitor. Had Harry's electronic transfer not gone through?

"The price this year is two million three hundred and fifty thousand dollars, Mr Carmichael," she said, without preamble.

"What?!" Harry spluttered. "Two million--?"

"-- three hundred and fifty." She shrugged. "Supply and demand, I'm afraid. We never knew there were quite so many multimillionaires awaiting our treatment."

"Can't you just... make more?"

"*If* we could increase production of our serum, then of course we would. But we can't. Our product is *strictly* limited." She tapped the monitor again with a perfect fingernail, raised an immaculately sculpted eyebrow. "Will that be a problem, Mr Carmichael?"

Harry tugged at his shirt collar. It would most certainly be a problem. It would damn near clean him out, and April would be none too pleased to find herself on a tight budget.

"No, no problem... um, I'll just need to move some funds around. If I could have... an hour?"

A thin smile. "Why don't I leave you for a while? Feel free to use the ultra secure NewGen WiFi. Just dial zero to get through to reception, when the balance has cleared."

Left alone, Harry sucked down a deep breath. Over two million! More than twice the usual price. Still, he had just enough, didn't he?

He didn't. He scanned his online account in rising disbelief. Where had all his money gone? To Harrods, to Boodles, and on a single night out with twenty of her friends at the Dorchester. April had taken out her birthday disappointment on an epic spending spree. It didn't matter what Harry did, he was short--well short. Perhaps if he sold his London flat?

But how long would that take? He had forty-five minutes left of the hour, and therefore eleven hours left of his annual treatment before he began to age. Already, he could feel his skin sag, his bones ache... His mind, playing tricks on him. But if not right now, if not precisely a year after his last treatment, then soon... *very* soon.

He looked up from the monitor, fists clenched. Somewhere beyond this office were the treatment rooms and the unseen labs, where the world's top geneticists engineered the precious anti-ageing serum. He'd already given NewGen this year's million; he was damn well going to get his treatment! Then he would start saving for next year. Tighten his belt, cut costs, increase prices... A round of redundancies, to trim what little fat there was. His profligate new wife included, perhaps.

His darting eyes settled on the glowing red LED of a CM 2000 HJ7 on the door opposite the one he'd entered by. The CM 2000 HJ7 was Carmichael's top of the range biometric lock, quantum enciphered, guaranteed unhackable. Only the very best, for NewGen!

For a moment, Harry sat perfectly still. He'd lost so many sales in failed demonstrations of the HJ7 that he'd had the software engineers hardcode his biometrics into every unit. The engineers were supposed to wipe the memory when the system was installed, but...

Harry quickly crossed the room, pressed a clammy thumb to the pad, bent to peer into the eye scanner.

The lock popped open with a satisfied *snick!*

He eased the door open, revealing a short corridor and a far more solid metal door beyond, emblazoned: "Authorised Lab Personnel Only". Sporting another CM 2000 HJ7.

Harry was going to get what he came for, one way or another.

The laboratory was brightly lit, and blissfully unoccupied. On a bench a shiny machine softly whirred. A centrifuge? As he hovered by the door, it spat out a familiar looking vial, pre-labelled with the NewGen logo.

Harry snatched it before metal jaws could whisk it up and away along a head height conveyor belt into another room, and turned to go, mission accomplished. Somehow he ended up spinning 360 degrees, staring again at the humming machine. What was the centrifuge, centrifuging? Where did the serum come from? Impelled by irresistible curiosity, he followed twin red tubes snaking along the edge of the workbench.

At the back of the room, on an oversized hospital air mattress that wheezed like an asthmatic smoker, lay a dusky white horse.

Harry shook his head, surprised. Immortality, from a horse? But then, horses were used for creating snake anti-venom, weren't they? This one looked rather emaciated, it was true; bones protruding from its rib cage, pressure sores splotching the white sheet it lay on. Still. Perhaps it was genetically modified? That would explain the centrifuge, the blood red colour of the tubes, the pale straw colour of the vial of anti-ageing serum.

But it wouldn't explain the odd stump emerging from the beast's forelock. A stump that looked suspiciously like--

"Yes," a soft, tired voice said. "I *am* a unicorn. *The* unicorn, if you prefer, since I'm the last one--on earth, at least." Two large brown eyes swivelled his way. "But you... who are you? You don't look like a scientist, or a doctor."

"I'm... I'm not," Harry agreed, mind swaddled in cotton wool. "I'm Harry."

"Well, Harry. Pleased to meet you. Now, if you could just undo my restraints?"

Harry blinked. Took in the heavy leather straps around the unicorn's four legs, the thicker collar around its slender neck. Reaching forward, he hesitated. "I, erm..."

"Release me!"

"*You're* the source of NewGen's treatment?"

"Of course," the unicorn said, long eyelashes fluttering. "Including the one you have in your pocket. That's *my* blood you just stole. Now, we don't have long. Start at the neck--"

"If I release you, what about next year?"

"What *about* what about next year?"

"If there's no anti-ageing serum, then...?"

"Ye gods! Must I make deals for my liberty? Haggle for my very existence? Bloody hell... Harry, do you really think my blood so feeble it only gives one extra year of life? Ah, that was the cleverest thing NewGen ever did; dilute my powers, allowing it to charge its customers annually. I guess I'm not the only being bled dry."

Harry blinked, tried to get to grips with a universe quite unlike the one he'd woken up in that morning. He was, he was fairly sure, a rational man. Did rational men find themselves talking to unicorns? "So... how long do the effects of your *un*diluted blood last, then?"

"Forever."

"Really?" Harry exclaimed. "Like... forever, forever?"

"Unicorns *never* lie."

Harry squinted. "And how do I know that's not a lie?"

"Untrusting humans! Very well. You may ask me any questions you like. Let my answers be the evidence of my truth. But please, can we get a *move* on?"

Harry thought for a moment. "How were you captured?"

The unicorn sighed. "I was enticed by a human female."

"A virgin?"

An equine snort. "How should I know? It's not something you can *smell*, it's not something you can detect from afar. All I can say is that she was awfully young, the witch."

"Witch?"

"*Veronica*. My captor and the founder of NewGen."

Harry groped in his memories for the brochure he'd read two decades earlier. "You mean, Dr Nick Flammel?"

"Hah! That ham! He's just an actor, a well paid front. It's the young girl that's behind it all; NewGen, and my pitiful plight. Her and her father, who captured me to cure his daughter's childhood illness. Well, I did far more than that. He probably would have tapped me myself had he known. Instead, the madman imprisoned me against the fear that his daughter's polio might return, that I might be needed again. He died before the true effects of my blood became apparent. It was his embittered and increasingly deranged daughter who did all of *this*."

Harry thought about it. He had some qualms about seeing an intelligent creature--mythical or not--tied up and drained of its blood. And while he didn't--couldn't--believe half of what the creature said, the very fact it said anything at all gave its supposed magical powers a fair bit of weight. What was undeniable was that the anti-aging serum he could no longer afford came from this beast. What did he have to lose?

Quickly, he unstrapped the thick leather restraints, starting at the feet. He ignored the neck-first instruction, reasoning that if a unicorn without a horn was going to attack him, it would have to be with the hooves, so best leave it bound elsewhere until he was done.

The unicorn didn't say anything, it just rolled its chestnut eyes.

The straps round the neck though were securely chained to either side of the bed, and resisted Harry's attentions. The padlocks were five pin tumblers, of course. No thumb print would unlock these. He caught the unicorn's eye as he struggled.

"Never mind," it sighed, "the binding charms have weakened over the years. I'll just need to gather all of my magical strength. And for that, Harry, you must remove the needles that drain my blood--and my powers."

Harry hesitated. "When do I...?"

"Gah! Man! You can hardly do it when the needle is still in, can you? Damn it, pull them out, upper leg first, put your mouth to the puncture wound, and suck. You *do* know how to suck, don't you?"

Harry winced. The needles were huge, more like knitting needles than anything he'd seen in a hospital before. He pressed on the first steel tube, tried his best to slide it out smoothly with his eyes closed. It clattered to the ground, trailing a red worm behind that cleared as the machine sucked up the remaining fluid. Harry bent over the forelock, lowered his lips to the bubble of bright red, and delicately sipped.

He gagged at the smell. At the warmth. At the very *thought*. But then something triggered a deeper, more primitive response. He crouched lower, wrapped his lips tightly against unicorn flesh, pulled hard on the wonderful, invigorating liquid, at the intoxicating--

"Not so hard!" the unicorn squealed. "And that's more than enough!"

Slowly, reluctantly, panting shallowly, Harry raised his face from deep in the short hairs of the unicorn's leg. He watched with eyes wide as the wound closed over, as the return tube emptied its cargo into the unicorn's other leg like a piece of red spaghetti being sucked into a hungry mouth. He shook his head to clear a shrill noise, before realising it was the centrifuge bleating an alarm.

"Quick!" the unicorn urged. "The second needle!"

Harry obeyed, resisting the temptation to bend and suck again, though no blood emerged from this vein, which quickly healed over just as the artery had.

The unicorn closed its eyes and shuddered, a deep breath filling the immense ribcage, which seemed less pronounced now, less gaunt. When it opened them again there was something intensely alive in them. Something rather scary.

"Thank you." Even its voice resonated with power. "Now, you'd best turn away while I extricate myself from this neck harness."

Harry, tingling all over, stood shock still.

"Suit yourself." There was a searing white light, light that echoed faintly with a "Goodbye, Harry," and then, as he blinked away tears and the afterimage of something no longer bound by the stiff, empty collar, something tall and graceful and splendid, something that sported a full, elegant spiral horn, he became aware that the something had morphed into something new, something small and dark had entered his dazzled field of vision. Small, dark, and angry. The unicorn had turned into... turned into...

Into a little girl, arms folded tightly over a charcoal gray, pint-sized business suit, her freckled face livid with rage.

"What have you DONE with my unicorn?" she spat.

Harry took a hasty step back at the fury in her voice.

"It's *Carmichael*, isn't it? The door sensors say so... Are you a fool, Mr Carmichael? Are you a cretin? Don't you realise that without my unicorn, there are no more NewGen treatments, for you, or for..." she trailed off, stared at him, stared up at his face. Self conscious, he licked his lips and tasted the salty tang of a stray drop of unicorn blood.

"Ah. Oh! I *see*. You have drunk from the fountain itself, haven't you Mr Carmichael? Pah! You're even more of a fool than I thought."

Harry frowned. Who was this... *girl*, who couldn't have been more than twelve, maybe thirteen at a pinch, to tell him he was a fool? How dare she?

And then it clicked: the young girl was the one the unicorn had talked about. Veronica. The founder of NewGen--a company recently celebrating its seventieth year of existence.

"You drank from the unicorn as well." It was half accusation, half dawning realisation.

"I did." She nodded. "At least I had good reason, or thought I did. Turns out I was just as much of a fool as you."

Two armed guards burst into the room, stubby black weapons held high. Veronica waved them impatiently away, waited until they'd left before turning back to Harry. He blanched under her hostile stare.

"What's so foolish about wanting to live forever?" he asked.

"Oh, you'll learn. And if you don't, I'll gladly tell you the next time we meet. And we will meet again, you and I. Again, and again, ad infinitum. There might be years--decades!--in between, but we two immortals, we can hardly avoid crossing paths, over and over. And every time we do, Mr Carmichael, I shall do my very *damnedest* to make you suffer!"

And with that, the octogenarian teenager turned and stalked away.

Liam Hogan is an award-winning speculative short story writer, with stories in Best of British Science Fiction and in Best of British Fantasy (NewCon Press). He volunteers at the creative writing charities Ministry of Stories, and Spark Young Writers. Sci-Fi collection: A Short

History of the Future (Northodox Press). Fantasy: Happy Ending Not Guaranteed (Arachne Press). More details at <u>http://happyendingnotguaranteed.blogspot.co.uk</u>

Book Reviews

The Review Team

All the Water in the World
Eiren Caffal

This is a cli-fi adventure full of thrills (and spills). Some of the action sequences are so full of drama, I found myself holding my breath, which is ironic as the world that we are introduced to by 13 year old protagonist Nonie is one that is under water – the glaciers have melted, New York city is almost deserted behind huge flood walls, built to keep the ocean at bay as the world rapidly succumbs to rising sea levels. Nonie and her family are camped out on the roof of the American Museum of Natural History. Here, as well as fighting for survival, they are trying to catalogue and save the artefacts and collections before they are lost to the floods.

Nonie, traumatised by the slow destruction of the modern world has developed a gift for predicting the approach of storms. And it is the crashing, devastating arrival of a superstorm – a hypercane – that forces her and her family to leave the relative safety of the museum and fight for survival as they head for higher ground. The tension in these moments as they try to paddle to safety in an ancient wooden canoe repatriated from the museum, is superbly crafted. Caffal successfully mirrors the threat to the little family's survival with the survival of the whole planet. The apocalyptic, relentless storm pushes everyone and everything to the edge of annihilation.

As you would expect in an apocalyptic scenario, there are a number of set pieces depicting how society is coping: loss of law and order, blockades, societal division. These sections are a little weak in the sense that this is how we 'expect' things to be in this type of novel: wild dogs, polluted water, cruel leaders etc etc. However, what I liked was the sense of hope provided by Caffal the end of her grim and gripping story. Without giving away spoilers, Nonie's affinity for the sea and its behaviour leads her to possible connections to further voyages in the name of science and discovery.

Underneath the danger of the advancing seas, this is a story about grief and loss, on a personal, environmental and historical level. And yet, it is also about resilience. And it leaves itself open for a great sequel.

A Hole in the Sky

Peter F. Hamilton

A new book by Peter F Hamilton is always a welcome event, though in recent years the wait times have been getting longer and longer. Fortunately, *A Hole in the Sky* will be followed rather swiftly (6 months) by the second book in its Arkship Trilogy and before 2026 is done the third and final instalment will land, just in time for Christmas.

Nothing in the accompanying details suggests this is YA, but it is. Young protagonists, Pred back language and the avoidance of the usual Hamilton-esque impenetrable science. He's reined in on the gore too, and given us a nice cute teeny love story. Which doesn't mean this isn't a good book – rather the opposite – but it does mean it's probably more accessible than most.

I'm a big fan of SF that's nominally focussed on a younger audience – Patrick Ness's *The Knife of Never Letting Go*, for instance, has imagination, pace and intrigue and *A Hole in the Sky* is arguably as strong. It's got quite few classic SF elements and masked them up into something new.

An arkship is hundreds of years out from Earth on its way to its second destination planet. The first turned out to have life on it that could potentially (and quickly) develop into an intelligent species, so the ship went on its way to a backup destination. But the encounter with the first planet triggered changes in the ship – a mutiny (some people wanted to turn back, apparently) triggered the destruction of advanced machines and forced social change into a more limited, agricultural society. But all is not well with the habitat, carved out of the interior of a massive asteroid, because a recent collision with something unknown has triggered a slow atmosphere leak. In a few years everyone will be dead, but the AI running the arkship, the Electric Captain, is carrying on as if nothing has changed. Young villager Hazel discovers the truth, though – and more besides – as she crosses the habitat to save the ship and her invalid brother, scheduled for death so he isn't a burden on the society Hazel increasingly questions.

At 400 pages, this is short by Peter F Hamilton standards, but it benefits from the reduced page count. His books can be sprawling affairs but this one is tight and focused – and very effective. Recommended.

Saltcrop
Yume Kitasei

A story about three sisters, one lost, two searching. Set somewhere unspecified, but probably the North American West Coast, this is a near future ravaged by climate change, where the crops are blighted and, increasingly, so are the people. The oldest sister, Nora, is missing. She'd been working for the megacorp Renewal, whose chemical solution to the ever-mutating blight has trapped rural communities in a cycle of famine, poverty and disease. Now she's on a mission to find 'clean' blight resistant crops, but she's disappeared.

The two remaining sisters abandon their plans and chase after Nora in a barely seaworthy boat, far up the coast where the air is cold and the nights are long. Every where they go, they just miss her, before hooking up with the seemingly helpful Jackson, who guides them even farther from home. Jackson, of course, is not what he seems, or at least not what the sisters hope he will be, and Nora remains tantalisingly out of reach.

Animals are developing mutations because of the chemicals used to combat the blight, and a deadly infection threatens to engulf the middle sister, Carmen. Both the inner world of the sister and the wider world is falling apart, and the stakes are high.

Saltcrop manages to be both plot driven and deeply character-led, which is impressive. The sisters are very different, and each of them gets a section to give their perspective. The youngest, Skipper, is distrustful of company and spends her time in the boatyard, barely contributing to the meagre family finances. Carmen has a nurse's job lined up and makes relationships easily: with Nora gone she's the breadwinner and main support to their grandmother, whose dementia is growing. Nora is a scientist and her quest has the potential to reveal the secrets behind Renewal and the blight. The sisters bicker, argue and fight, but they have a deep mutual respect. Although that doesn't readily translate into trust. Carmen, in particular, nearly sacrifices everything to find her sister, including letting her job drift away and keeping the passage of her disease from everyone, which nearly kills her. And, as they all discover, this is not a safe world, and Renewal doesn't reveal its secrets without a fight.

The worldbuilding in this novel is excellent, though not always subtle, and highly credible. The sisters are believable too, for instance in the way they fail to properly communicate with each other, leading to all sorts of problems, and the novel's take on corporate greed, ruthlessness and indifference has uneasy echoes in real life. The setting and the planet's future may be bleak but many of the people in this novel are kind and selfless and there's a cheerful optimism running throughout, despite the odds being very much against a happy ending. But don't bet against three stubborn sisters on a selfless mission.

Aerth
Deborah Tomkins

Aerth is a novella set on two alternate Earths both orbiting the sun at opposite ends of their orbit (I recall a Gerry Anderson film – *Journey to the Other Side of the Sun* – covering a similar idea as well as the more recent *Another Earth*). Aerth (the planet) is a green world with a declining population, working on democratic principles with a 'do no harm' ideal. Young Magus is impatient and a bit too self-centred for that world and when the opportunity comes to fly to the newly discovered Urth on the other side of the sun he takes it, leaving his girlfriend Tilly behind. He's part of the first and only mission to Urth and is the only survivor after crash landing There he finds a technologically advanced, overpopulated and polluted Earth, an exaggerated version of our own planet. Initially he's feted and treated as an interesting curiosity, funded by the UK Government. But eventually the crowds and politicians begin to tire of him and he starts to pine fo the planet he left behind. Be careful what you wish for, seems to be the message, and this journey towards self-awareness drives the story.

Aerth isn't perfect: there's an ice age coming and the population is being decimated by a mystery virus. Urth is noisy, overcrowded and dangerous – increasingly too hot rather than too cold. Magnus never seems happy there, and as his fortunes decline conspiracies take hold: is he really an astronaut? Is there really another Urth like planet, unseen at the other side of the sun? There's a *Man who Fell to Earth* feel about all this – Marcus is a stranger in a strange land, rejected, forlorn and unable to get home.

As with most good tales you can take this on a number of levels. You can drift along with the seductive prose, follow the narrative literally or seek hidden meaning, which in this case is about both personal growth and our capacity for self destruction. We're invited to choose ourselves between the two alternative Earths – both, in their own ways leading to ultimate decline – and consider our planetary role: custodians or exploiters.

This story makes you think, but it's also a bit frustrating. Maybe it's the novella length, but we never really get under the skin of Marcus, and his relationship with Tilly (on both worlds) is crying out for more development. Despite this detachment from the characters and the overly familiar doppleganger Earth trope, there's enough here to intrigue and raise questions, if not enough to properly explore them. But an interesting read nonetheless and a qualified recommendation.

Every Version of You
Grace Chan

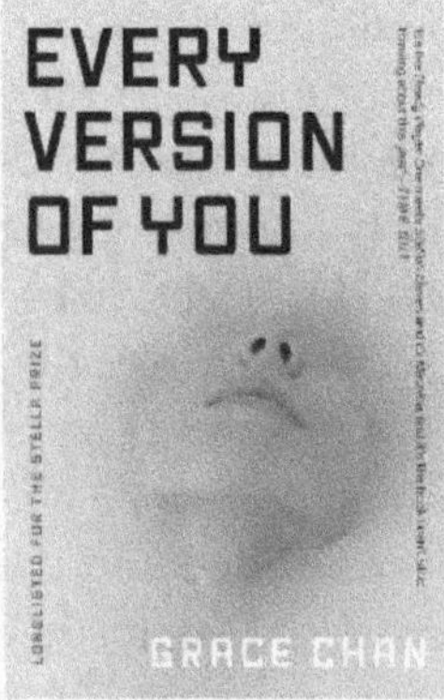

Every Version of You is a debut novel set in Australia. It's a competent, thought provoking narrative that's definitely worth a read It's a near future cautionary tale with a cyberpunk vibe. It all sounds frighteningly plausible, too, at least in initial setup. Increasingly everybody logs on to an immersive world, allowing their bodies to rot in sad, darkened apartments. Ultimately, the technology allows for permanent digital upload with no need to maintain corporeal bodies. So most of the world disappears into big server blocks leaving just a few who can't – or won't – sever ties with the real world.

So far so *Black Mirror*. But it's the characters and the human dilemmas that drive this narrative and the protagonist – Tao-Yi – has some impossible choices to make. She's got a mother who refuses to engage in the new online world, and as physical infrastructure declines from underuse (the airports all close, for instance, and the streets (and shops) are empty), she's increasingly dependent on her daughter. Plus there's Tau-Yi's husband, Navin, who leaves his disability behind and redefines himself in the online world. Does Taiu-Yi join him, or increasingly make excuses for her heel-dragging?

Are the uploaded people the same? To a large extent they can now define their own realities and have a different relationship with life, death and the stages in between so almost certainly not. Are they happier? Are they even human?

Naviin doesn't need sleep any more and his brain speeds up, unfettered by the constraints of physicality. Tau-Yi can barely keep up with him and she increasingly finds the balance of their relationship shifting, But she's got an incentive to join him: she, like her mother, has a degenerative brain condition that online immortality would cure. But at what expense?

As directions of travel go, this one's scary, and the thought of a transcendent humanity entirely dependent on massive server banks in the desert heat tended by robots sounds disturbingly fragile. Plus the world they create – of boundless possibility – is instead an insular one of pointless circularity. Sounds like hell.

Recommended.

Opposite World
Elizabeth Anne Martins,

I'm beginning to expect Flame Tree Press to hit me with something quirky and different. They don't always hit the mark, but when they do they're edgy, thoughtful and engaging, with stories from writers who may not be too familiar but often have an interesting take on the world.

Opposite World, the second novel from Elizabeth Anne Martins, fits neatly into that pattern. It's an articulate near future *Black Mirror*-style take on loss and memory in a high the thriller package. Pip's mother dies and she's brought up by her father in a backwoods cabin in Washinton State. She's shielded from tech – no computers, no internet – though it becomes clear her father used to work in IT. But as she gets older, gets married and moves out, the world that her father was trying to protect her from comes crashing in. Specifically, he tells her to avoid The Reverie Cloud: a virtual reality programme designed to tap into past memories. But it turns out to be much more than that. Inevitably, Pip is sucked in, looking for answers about her mother's death, and finds herself in great danger. Plus there's a blurring of reality and memory until Pip finds she really can't trust either.

On one level it's a thriller, because Pip's the key to something lost and it's important, to her father at least, that that *stays* lost. So there's a bad guy (Victor) a chase, a fight and all the usual thriller stuff. On another level, it's another warning about new technology and maybe a nod to the frustrations and addictions of the virtual world. But at the heart of the story, at the heart of every good story, is character, and Pip's growth throughout the novel is central to its success.

And it does succeed. The writing is very rich but readable and the narrative reaches a satisfying but mildly unexpected conclusion. The pacing's a little uneven and I wasn't sure about the extended epilogues but it held my interest throughout, though some of the time jumps and memory fragments were disorientating. Also there was a character tor two I couldn't quite see the point of – the husband, Farley, for instance, who was both unconvincing and unnecessary. But Pip's compulsion to uncover the truth and her dive down a dangerous rabbit hole are strong drivers of tension and suspense, and the positives far outweigh the negatives. It's quite cinematic too – I can see this being picked up by one of the streamers.

Spiderlight
Adrian Tchaikovsky

Yet another Adrian Tchaikovsky book to fill my shelves, and at this rate I'm going to need a new shelf just to keep up with him. He's certainly prolific – though in this instance this isn't an entirely new work: it was first published in serialised form rather obscurely in *Aethernet* magazine in 2013, then later picked up by Tor in 2016, so this one's got legs. Eight of them, I guess, because spiders play a key role in this fast moving snarky-comedy fantasy tale of the light and the dark and shades in between.

Dion is a Priestess of Armes, the righteous religion of the Light, on a holy mission to destroy the Dark once and for all by tracking the evil Dark Lord Darvezian to his lair and killing him with the fang of a giant spider. The only way to reach the Dark Castle, though, is to follow the spider path, which means making a deal with the spiders. She's accompanied by a thief, a wizard a swordsman and a warrior woman, whose faith in her faith ranges from contempt to mild acceptance, which leads to much amusement and some tension as the novel unfolds. The story, though, belongs to the spider they bring along as a guide, transformed into something not quite human by the wizard. Nth (or Enth as he becomes) has a transformative journey through this story, and the book is probably best viewed as his story arc.

It's all standard fantasy trope setup, from the Dark Lord and his Doomsayer enforcers to the motley ragtag band of heroes with the classic fight between light and dark, but if you're expecting Trhaikovsky to play that hand straight I suspect you haven't read any of this other books. He subverts the tropes deliciously, with some satisfying revelations at the denouement, and any pompous high fantasy nonsense is firmly brought down to earth with wit and charm.

I loved this book. It's light on its feet and moves at pace. Sure, the story gives us what we're expecting, really, and the characters rarely surprise us, but that's not really the point here. If I have a minor quibble it's that the development of the ostensible protagonist, Dion, gets rather lost in favour of the humanising of the spider, Enth, and I would really have liked to see much more, later on, from her point of view as her faith unravels and her perceptions of her travelling companions alter with familiarity. She's arguably the least developed of all the major characters, sadly.

Great cover too.